To the real Orla. Both of them.

CHAPTER 1

It was Friday the thirteenth of August, and the first day of Orla Perry's summer holiday. Tall for her twelve years with straggly red hair and green eyes that sometimes looked blue, Orla was pretty excited about what was to be her first real holiday since she was nine. Her brothers, Richard and Tom – fifteen and ten respectively – not so much. The bickering had started before they'd left London – caught up in rush-hour traffic because, all but one of them agreed, Richard had spent too long doing his hair.

Now the five of them – Mum and Richard in the front, Orla and Tom in the back, and Dave the dog wedged in with the luggage – were sat in a steamed-up hatchback in a fifteen-mile tailback somewhere west of Exeter on the A38. Richard's surfboard was strapped to the roof, Lady Gaga was on the radio and the windscreen wipers were waving like festival fans. Outside, the sky was the same colour as the road and a fine drizzle filled the air like static.

"Are we nearly there yet?" whined Tom. He'd been

asking the same question every five minutes for four and three-quarter hours and clearly still thought it was funny.

"Shut up," growled Mum. "Ask me that one more time and I'll drive us straight back to London."

"Are we nearly there yet?" chorused Tom and Richard in unison.

"Ungrateful swines," muttered Mum.

"What I don't get is why we've left a perfectly good house in a modern city to drive all the way to Cornwall to stay in a shack in the woods," said Tom. He had a practical approach to life.

"It's not a shack in the woods," said Mum.

"Yes, it is," retorted Richard. "I looked it up. There's some woods, and a shack."

"It's a traditional Cornish cottage in a peaceful location near the charming village of Poldevel, and only five minutes' walk from a secluded beach," recited Mum.

"It's a shack in the woods miles from anywhere," insisted Richard.

"It's a *free* shack in the woods," corrected Mum. "And it was very kind of Mrs Spark to lend it to us."

"Who exactly is this Mrs Spark?" asked Richard.

"She's an old friend of Mrs Cottrall's," said Mum.

"Mrs Cottrall is weird," muttered Tom. "I bet her friend's traditional Cornish shack is weird too."

"Mrs Cottrall is not weird," said Mum. "She's a church warden."

"Do we even know if there's electricity in this shack?" asked Richard a little later.

Mum sighed as the traffic came to a halt again. "She said there's an Internet router, so there must be."

"Only Wi-Fi is going to make this week bearable," Richard warned.

Orla smiled and gazed out of the window. The sheep looked like crash-landed clouds, and she liked the weird hills, with their Mohican haircuts of trees. Most of all, she loved the sensation of travel – the fizzing excitement of heading into the unknown. She opened her backpack and ran her hands over her kit: the penknife her dad had given her, her pencil case, a silent whistle for Dave the dog that he resolutely ignored, a torch, a notebook, a first aid kit and some plastic gloves she'd grabbed at a petrol station because it was better to have things and not need them than need things and not have them.

And Malasana.

She felt a twinge of embarrassment, followed by a rush of guilt, as she squeezed the old rag doll. Her dad had given her Malasana on the day she was born, and even though she knew she was too old to be cuddling a doll, Malasana, with her crazy black hair and her gypsy dress, was an old friend, and Orla was certain that she brought her good luck.

In the back, perched atop a shifting stack of suitcases and groceries, Dave was planning his move. Eight years old, with short legs and an even shorter temper, his job was head of household security, specializing in close protection and threat detection. No one else in the car had ever appreciated that. To them, the grizzled black and white Jack Russell terrier was a grumpy pet who gave postmen a hard time. And wouldn't stay put in the back of cars.

Dave crept forward, keeping his head down. Incursions into the passenger cabin of the car were always tricky operations, hampered by angry protests from hostile civilians. One option was to jump. The other was to creep, on the off chance he wouldn't be noticed. He went with option two.

"*Muuummm,*" cried Tom. "Dave's making a move."

"Dave," barked Mum. "Get in the back."

"Get back, Dave," shouted Richard.

Orla smiled. She knew how this would end.

Dave ignored everybody. He clambered over Tom's shoulders, dropped onto the seat, then climbed over Orla's lap to reach the window.

"He's farted," wailed Tom.

Orla scratched him behind the ear. "I think he's just excited to be going on holiday," she said.

Predictably, they got lost. Orla woke up – with Dave still on her lap – to hear Mum and Richard arguing over directions and thunder that exploded like bombs. Outside, blue bolts of lightning pierced the wet, black night and hard rain fell like nuts and bolts on the roof of the car.

"We have absolutely no idea where we're going," confessed Mum. She sounded tired.

"It's left," said Orla, wondering how she could be so certain.

Richard spun to glare at her. "Don't confuse matters."

"It's left," she insisted. "Then left again, right at the fork, straight down the hill and left again immediately after the bridge."

"You sound very certain about that," said Mum slowly, studying Orla in the rear-view mirror as though she'd just heard a squirrel quote Shakespeare. "How can you be so sure?"

Orla shrugged. "Dunno. But I bet I'm right."

She was too.

They knew when they saw the tiny, hand-painted sign in the hedge. Richard turned and gave Orla a *how the hell?* look. Orla smiled. The red paint spelled out Konnyck Vean, and an arrow pointed down a muddy track through a tunnel of trees that swayed back and forth like great black sails ripped loose from a mast.

"Looks like a painting by a psychopath," observed Tom, as lightning flashed and thunder followed. No one disagreed.

They rolled carefully down the rutted track until the car headlights picked out a white cottage in a clearing. Then they sat and stared for a few moments.

"This is it, kids," said Mum. "A traditional Cornish cottage in a secluded location. *Not* a shack."

"It looks like the sort of house where people are murdered," said Richard.

"Don't be so dramatic," chided Mum.

Dave was coiled like a spring, ready to leap into action the moment anyone opened a door. Orla was first to oblige, and he could hear their cries of indignation as he slipped into the night, nose close to the ground. They could moan all they liked about muddy paws, but the first priority of a security professional when arriving at a new base was to check the entire area for threats. And wee up the odd tree.

It took twenty minutes to lug everything into the cottage. Orla thought it was amazing, with its dark slate floor, rough plastered walls, antique cooker and plastic wall clock that looked like it had stopped in 1972. Creaky wooden stairs led up to three bedrooms and a bathroom with a cast-iron

12

bathtub, a fluffy pink mat and a loose window that rattled in the gale.

As she was admiring the retro vibe, Tom dashed past.

"This room's mine," he yelled.

"No way," protested Orla. "I get the single room because I'm the only girl."

Tom threw himself onto the bed and shook his head. "Sorry, mate. Too late." A sudden thunderclap made him jump, and the lights flickered.

Richard appeared. "I'm taking this room," he announced, "so get off my bed, squirt."

"He's not on your bed," growled Orla, blocking the doorway. "He's on mine."

Richard pushed past her, scouting the room for plug sockets. "You two can share," he said. "I need privacy." He looked up at them in mock surprise, his floppy hair falling across his face. "Still here, children? Jog on."

"Orla!" It was Mum, calling from the bottom of the stairs. "I'm not letting that filthy dog into this house until you've rubbed him down."

Orla frowned. "Why me?"

"Because you let him out of the car. Go and fetch the dog towel from the boot."

It should have taken Orla a few seconds to find Dave's grotty old towel and return to the cottage, but that would have meant missing the show. Instead, she stood in the pouring rain, watching the lightning and grinning like a kid at a firework display. She'd hoped there would be barn owls or tawny owls in these woods, but no owl with an ounce of wisdom would be out tonight. That would be good news for the rabbits. The soggy rabbits. A long, low rumble of thunder rolled across the sky, fleeing a whiplash crack that seemed to knock the leaves from the trees.

That, decided Orla, deserved a round of applause, and it was only when she felt the cold water running down her spine that she remembered the task in hand. She popped the boot and grabbed the towel, and as she slammed the hatch another flash lit up the clearing. For a millisecond, Orla was certain she saw a hooded figure watching her. Then, as the thunder trundled down the valley, it was gone.

All was quiet but for the drumming of the rain and the swish of the trees. Orla frowned into the darkness for a few moments, then shook her head.

"Trick of the light," she decided, and without a backwards glance she went indoors.

By the time Dave was decontaminated, the bedroom dispute had been settled. Mum had one double room, the boys the other and Orla took the coveted single room at the front. But there was now a much bigger problem.

"The bloody Wi-Fi doesn't work," wailed Richard.

A crack of thunder rattled the windows.

"Maybe the storm knocked out the signal," said Mum wearily.

"I'm going to die," said Richard. He turned away from the blinking router, looking plaintively at Mum, Tom and Orla. "I'm serious," he said. "I can't live for a week in the woods without Wi-Fi."

Mum poured herself a glass of wine. "Don't be ridiculous," she said. "Think of this as a digital detox."

Luckily, the TV worked, in a fuzzy, three-channel, 1970s kind of way. They ate supermarket pizza and then, exhausted, went to bed. Outside, the lightning flashed, the thunder growled and the storm thrashed like a trapped shark in the trees.

CHAPTER 2

Orla woke at 5.37 a.m. and spent a few delicious moments wondering where on earth she was. The mattress was lumpy and she could see woodchip wallpaper, a tasselled lampshade, and grey light coming through the curtainless window. Then she remembered: she was on holiday. In Cornwall. Yes!

She sprang out of bed and looked out of the tiny window. It had stopped raining, which was a good sign. The birds would be out, and they always sang louder after a storm. She dressed, picked Malasana off the bed and placed her carefully in her backpack, and then crept down the corridor to the boys' room.

"Tom," she hissed. "Wake up."

No response. She flicked his ear, eliciting a grunt.

"Wake up, Tom."

Still no response, so she tugged on his eyebrows until his eyelids cracked.

"Get lost, you crazy witch," he mumbled.

"Get up," insisted Orla, poking him in the ribs. "Let's go exploring."

"It's still last night, you lunatic," he groaned, rolling away from her.

Orla turned her attention to her elder brother. "Wake up, Richard!"

"Go away," he hissed.

"Surf's pumping, dude. Grab your board, man."

Richard pushed his sleep mask onto his forehead, propped himself up on his elbows and gave his sister a menacing look. "Go. Away. Now," he growled.

Orla shrugged. Their loss, not hers.

She grabbed the yellow sou'wester she'd bought from a charity shop for fifty pence and tiptoed downstairs to find Dave. His basket had been placed beside the fireplace to make him feel at home, so he'd slept on the sofa, like he did at home. He was flat on his back with his legs in the air and he opened one eye as Orla approached.

"Get up, dog," she whispered. "We're going exploring."

Dave yawned, rolled over and scratched his ear. He enjoyed dawn patrols. And he needed a wee.

Outside, the morning twilight had paled into a low, grey overcast of fast-moving cloud pushed by the wind like a dirty mop. Leaves, twigs and broken branches were scattered across the clearing like sprinkles on a cheap cake, and deep brown puddles lay like cold gravy along the track. Beyond, over a gurgling stream and across a broken stone wall, a swampy-looking field climbed away towards the sky.

"Dave, can you believe we've got this place to ourselves for a whole week?" Orla gasped. "It's going to be brilliant."

She peered up into the trees. Her dad had once told her that some people never noticed birds, just like some people couldn't see colours. How could you not notice birds – especially here in this ancient Cornish wood?

Except, well, there *weren't* any birds. Not even a blackbird. How odd, thought Orla. Maybe the storm had blown them away.

She lowered a welly-clad foot into the stream, then pulled it back. Too deep. But perfect for damming. As she headed downstream, Dave ran ahead, zigzagging through the wet ferns, sniffing like a bloodhound seeking a long-gone fugitive and stopping every few seconds to mark his territory.

There was something very odd here, but he couldn't put a paw on exactly what. All he knew was that nothing smelled right, and that was rarely a good sign.

"C'mon, dog," called Orla. She had jumped the stream and was waiting for him on the other side.

Dave wondered if she had noticed the lack of birdlife. The wind was thumping the trees and they were creaking in complaint, but he couldn't hear a single tweet.

"Make the jump," urged Orla.

Dave ignored her. He sensed a clear and present danger, but he couldn't locate it. His hackles rose like a porcupine and a low growl rumbled in his throat, matching the rumbling he could feel beneath his paws. He heard a dull groan, accompanied by a popping sound, like an oil rig breaking its tethers.

"What's your problem, dog?" called Orla, jumping from the bank to a midstream rock. "Scared of getting your paws wet?"

She jumped back to the far bank, turning to show Dave how easy it was, but instead of following her he went full-on, scrapyard-mongrel berserk, barking with the ferocity of the world's last living dog faced by an army of zombie postmen. Loud enough to wake the entire neighbourhood – had there been any neighbours. Definitely urgent enough to make Orla turn. Scary enough to make her jump back across the stream, and just enough to save her life as, with a monstrous gasp, fifty tonnes of oak tree crashed to earth, its roots tearing a vast disc of soil from the ground, its branches snapping like a giant's bones and its leaves sighing like a million ghosts.

And then, as the last clods of earth thudded to the ground, it was over.

Silence returned to the wood. Orla looked at Dave. Dave closed his eyes, took a deep breath and shook himself. That had been too close for comfort.

The mighty tree lay like a slain emperor. Orla hopped over the stream and rubbed her hands gently along the oak's cracked green skin.

"'My name is Ozymandias, king of kings'," she whispered. "'Look on my works, ye Mighty, and despair!'" She threw a glance at Dave. "Percy Bysshe Shelley wrote that."

Dave stared at her. He had no idea what she was talking about. She jumped back across the stream, bent down and hugged him. "Well spotted, dog," she whispered. She straightened and, hands on hips, inspected the fallen giant. "Let's look for birds' nests."

The bark was wet and slippery and it took Orla a couple of attempts to pull herself up onto the trunk. She clambered along, high above the stream, pushing through the boughs of what, until a minute ago, had been the very top of a mighty tree. Suddenly, a single ray of sunlight punched through the clouds. Arrow-straight from heaven, it seared through the foliage like a spotlight and hit something hidden in the furthermost branches. There was a dazzling red flash, and then the beam was snuffed out by the overcast.

Dropping to her hands and knees, Orla crept towards

the flash, slithering through the leaves like a tree snake. By now she was almost at the top, or rather the end, where, dangling from a fork, was something that looked like a large, brown caterpillar with black feet. Orla reached for it, grabbed it and felt its weight, its unexpected sharpness, in her dirty hands. She gazed at it for a long time, her mouth sagging in wonder. Then she said, "Oh. My. God."

It was a necklace – a complicated arrangement of three strands of stones almost as long as her arm. Back on solid ground, Orla knelt beside the stream and carefully lowered the jewels into the cold water. All but one – the one that had flashed – were encased in a thick layer of dark green lichen, but as she washed them, their true colour began to shine through. The deepest, darkest red, like blood. They had to be rubies, right? What other jewels were red? Garnets? Topaz? But they weren't especially precious – surely not enough to warrant being mounted in gold. And she was certain that these rocks were mounted in gold – washed in the stream, those black caterpillar feet were gleaming yellow. And there was something else. In the middle of the top strand was a sort of medallion – maybe twice as big as a two-pound coin. She rubbed it and it glittered.

"Dave," she breathed. Her hands were trembling, her head was giddy and her heart was beating so fast she thought she might faint. "We've found treasure."

* * *

"Orl-aaa!"

The shout snapped her out of her trance. It was Tom.

"Should have been here earlier," muttered Orla, moving Malasana aside so she could coil the stones into her backpack. Family rules probably stated that she should show Mum her discovery, but Orla knew exactly how that would go. Firstly, there would be a tsunami of questions concerning the how, why, when, where and what the hell. Secondly, Mum would insist that the necklace be taken to the police, and that would be that. No harm, reasoned Orla, in keeping her treasure secret until she had the time to conduct her own investigations.

"Orl-aaaa!"

She jogged back up the valley, emerging in the clearing beside the cottage.

"Where the hell have you been?" asked Tom. "Breakfast is ready, and..." He trailed off, suddenly noticing how dishevelled his sister was. Her jeans were muddy and tree-stained, and there was a trickle of blood – a scratch from a twig – running down her face. "What the hell have you been doing?"

Orla shrugged. "Oh. A massive tree fell over, but otherwise, not much."

CHAPTER 3

That night, the nightmares started.

Mum had been predictably furious at Orla for messing up her clothes on the first day of the holiday. Richard had given her his usual look of utter disapproval, and Tom still wanted to know what the hell she'd been doing; but with the valley now out of bounds – too dangerous, thought Mum – she couldn't even show him the stream, let alone the fallen oak.

The necklace was hidden under her mattress, wrapped in a carrier bag. She'd noticed what looked like disappointment on Malasana's face as she'd stashed it.

"OK, I know it's not the best hiding place," Orla had hissed. "But for the time being it'll have to do."

She pulled on clean jeans and a T-shirt and gave the rag doll a hard look. "Guard it with your life," she ordered, then dashed downstairs to where the others were waiting to embark on an exciting day out.

Mum had decided that the crappy weather precluded

a trip to the beach and had announced instead that they should visit the Eden Project – a collection of giant, jungle-filled golf balls in a valley somewhere north of St Austell.

As days out went, it was deeply rubbish, mainly because every other family on holiday in Cornwall had decided that the crappy weather precluded a trip to the beach. So, rather like the day before, they spent most of Saturday in a traffic jam.

Everyone noticed how distant Orla seemed all day, and everyone assumed she was sulking because Mum had told her off. But she wasn't upset at all. She just couldn't trust herself not to blurt out that she'd found a priceless (and it *had* to be priceless) ruby necklace hidden in a tree that had crashed down right beside her as though it had been waiting all along to reveal its secret.

On the way home, she turned round to look at Dave, sitting disgruntledly in the boot. He looked back, disgruntledly. She could trust him to keep the secret, and the others were ignoring her, which worked just fine. And they had chips for tea, which was a result.

At 9 p.m. Orla said goodnight and climbed the creaking stairs to bed.

Hours later, she was woken by a crow. It was sitting on the window ledge, cawing insistently and tapping on the glass with its black beak. She climbed out of bed and went to the window, delighted to see a bird. The crow looked at her, first with one glittering eye and then the other, before flying down to the unkempt grass in the clearing. Orla watched it watching her, then flinched as he flew back up to the window and tapped hard on the glass.

"OK," she said. "I'm coming."

She was outside before she realized she'd forgotten to wake Dave, but there was no time to go back. The crow was in a hurry, and he wanted her to follow. The clearing looked somehow different from yesterday. The trees seemed healthier and greener. The detritus left after Friday night's storm had gone, and their car was missing. She hurried after the crow, following the stream down the valley towards the beach she had not yet seen. Soon they'd pass the fallen oak, she thought. Except there was no fallen oak.

Then there were no more trees – just the light grey sky falling into a dark grey sea. There was a girl running on the beach, her green dress dragging on the sand, her red hair streaming in the wind, her hand pressed to a wound in her side and an urgency to her flight, as though she was chasing something. Or being chased.

Suddenly, Orla heard shouting – angry and violent – as a mob of men came charging along the shore. She saw the flash of knives, the knob of a wicked-looking club, and she wished she'd brought Dave. He was small, but he was mean, and she missed having him by her side. Especially now. But the men ran past her as though she wasn't there, their breath pungent with alcohol and tobacco, their boots thumping on the wet sand. They wanted the girl in the green dress, but she was too fast. She skipped over black rocks, onto the cliff path, and disappeared.

The mob slowed, then stopped, bending to grab their knees and catch their breath as a single horseman clad in a long coat and a three-pointed hat came galloping along the beach. He wheeled his sweating mare at the rocks and then stared right at Orla.

"Damn you, Pedervander Mazey!" he yelled. "Damn you to hell."

And then Orla woke up.

It was still dark. Feeling a bit dizzy, she climbed out of bed and inspected her feet. They weren't sandy. She crossed to the window. There was no crow, and the car was parked exactly where Mum had left it.

She flopped back down on the bed, staring at the cracks in the ceiling as though the answers were hidden within them. Because the questions were piling up: the mysterious figure she'd seen in the storm; the necklace; and now this eerily vivid dream. They had to be linked. Or did they? What on earth was going on in this weird place?

Orla let out an exasperated sigh, grabbed her notebook and pencil case from her backpack and wrote down the name the horseman had screamed.

Peter van der Mazie.

CHAPTER 4

Orla had eaten breakfast by the time the rest of the family emerged, one by one, in yawns and slippers.

"What are you drawing?" asked Mum, pouring hot water onto a green tea bag.

"A crazed mob of murderous peasants," replied Orla.

"Nice," said Mum.

Tom flopped down at the kitchen table. "I'm so tired," he moaned. "Crazy dreams all night."

"About a five-star hotel with an indoor pool and free Wi-Fi?" asked Richard.

Tom shook his head. "Not that crazy. I dreamed about a shipwreck. It was pretty cool actually." He fished in his dressing gown pocket and tossed something small and red onto the table. "What do you think that is? I found it under my bed."

Mum peered over her glasses at the object – a small parcel of scarlet felt stitched closed with green thread.

"Looks like a bit of potpourri," she guessed. "Put it back."

"Later," said Tom, booting up his Switch. "So what are we doing today?"

"You lot are going out exploring," said Mum. "I've got a ton of lesson plans to sort out for next term and I would appreciate some peace and quiet."

Richard glanced through the rain-streaked window. "No chance," he muttered.

"Why don't you go on a birdwatching expedition?" persisted Mum.

"There aren't any birds," said Orla. "It's weird."

"There are always birds," argued Mum. "Some people just don't see them."

"That's Dad's line," said Tom.

"If your father were here he'd have the three of you out on a ten-mile hike," she muttered.

"But he's not," said Orla. "He's in Africa."

"Sunny, warm Africa," added Tom. "So unfair."

"Can't be helped." Mum shrugged. "Why don't you take Dave for a walk?"

Tom didn't look up from his Switch. "Nope."

Mum groaned. She looked at Orla. "Why can't you draw something nice?"

"Like what?"

"Like some horses. Or a still life."

Orla gave a little sigh. Mum dreamed about having a

daughter who loved museums and spa days and shopping trips, but that was all it was: a vain and foolish dream.

She zipped up her pencil case, closed her notebook and put on the yellow sou'wester. "Let's go, dog," she said, pulling on her wellies and grabbing her backpack.

The rain was worse than ever: a spiteful barrage of cold nails driven into her face by a hammering wind. But there were mysteries to solve, whatever the weather.

She stopped by Ozymandias in spite of Mum's ban and touched him to make sure he was really there, before pressing on to the rain-pocked beach. It was exactly as it had looked in her dream, except without the fleeing girl and crazed mob. To the right, high black crags with boulders the size of bungalows at their feet. To the left, more rocks and a grassy slope that grew up quickly to become a cliff, and a fist of granite as big as a church that punched across the sand to the sea. Straight ahead, the wind-whipped Atlantic, thumping over and over onto the empty beach. There should have been sandpipers and turnstones and terns and herring gulls all along the shore, thought Orla. Instead, nothing.

Nothing except another human being, here very recently. Whoever it was had written their name in the sand. Happy to know she wasn't the only one who didn't mind the rain, Orla wandered over to inspect the scrawl. It was much,

much more than an autograph – a complicated geometrical pattern carved carefully into the beach, its seaward edge already licked by the rising tide.

From down here, it was impossible to see exactly what the artist had created, so Orla walked back up the beach to gain some height, hopping from one boulder to the next, leaping across rock pools and climbing higher and higher until the design became clear. A five-armed star in a circle of brown seaweed – a pentacle. Chunks of salt-sodden driftwood had been placed at the points, and a boulder the size of a fridge stood dead centre. There were symbols – weird squirls and half-arrows and zigzags – that looked vaguely threatening, but not as threatening as the words in plain English scratched across the bottom.

GO HOME LITTLE WITCH.

"That's not very friendly," muttered Orla.

Suddenly, Dave was on alert. He was staring up at the cliff, making the low, rumbling growl he used when his suspicions were aroused. Orla followed his eyeline.

There was a hooded figure on the clifftop. Standing there. Watching.

Orla waved. "Hellooo," she called.

The figure simply stared back.

Orla felt a jab of irritation, washed over by a wave of curiosity. Was this the shadow she'd spotted lurking in the lane last night? Had this person scratched the message in the sand? And who, exactly, was it meant for? These mysteries needed solving right now.

She whistled for Dave and, without waiting for him to catch up, set off up the zigzag path in pursuit.

Dave watched her for a moment, shaking his head in frustration and disbelief. The girl had gone charging into a potentially hostile situation with no plan. Probably hadn't even done a risk assessment. He sighed and sprinted after her.

The figure had disappeared by the time they reached the top of the cliff, but Dave knew exactly where it had gone. The scent trail led through the bushes, doubling back into the valley where the fallen tree lay. He gave a low woof to let Orla know.

"Good work, dog." She nodded. "Let's go."

Dave stuck his nose to the ground and took off. Down the slope, across the stream and up the cliff path, glancing back every now and then to make sure Orla was following. He was close now, so he slowed to a wolf-like prowl until the target came into view.

It was a girl, dressed head to toe in black like a Victorian widow and sat on what looked like an ancient rock shelter.

There was mud on the hem of her dress and her boots, and silver rings on her fingers. The hair spilling from her hoody was the colour of rooks; her lips were the colour of blood. Dave went full hedgehog, the hair on his back standing on end, and a low, menacing growl rumbled in his throat.

Then Orla arrived.

"Why are you following me?" demanded the girl.

She's a goth, thought Orla. An actual goth. "You were stalking me," she replied.

The goth laughed without humour. She looked about fourteen, but it was difficult to tell. "Nice try. But you actually followed me." Her eyes dropped to Dave, whose tactical response had escalated from growling to showing his teeth. "Is he likely to attack?"

"Depends," said Orla. "He'll do a risk assessment first."

The goth drew her legs up onto the rock. "Why are you here?"

"Like I said: because you've been stalking me," said Orla. "You were outside my house on Friday night, and now you're writing rude messages in the sand. Are you trying to scare me?"

The goth sighed. "I wasn't outside your house and I didn't write the message in the sand. Someone else did, and don't flatter yourself. It wasn't meant for you."

"So who was it meant for?"

"Me," said the goth.

"Are you a witch?"

"Someone seems to think so."

"Who?"

The goth gave Orla a long look, ignoring the rain dripping from her nose. "Best not to get involved," she said at last.

"Why?"

"How old are you?"

"Twelve," said Orla. "Thirteen on the twenty-first of November."

"You're too young to play this game. Take your psycho dog, enjoy your holiday, and then go back to wherever you came from. And don't forget to try the fudge. It's very good."

"Are you in trouble?" asked Orla.

"We're done here," said the goth. She jumped off the rock, gave Dave a wary look and strode away.

Orla hurried after her. Persistence always paid off. "I'm Orla Perry, by the way," she called. "What's your name?"

The goth kept walking, her dress catching on the gorse. She didn't reply.

"I think we should talk," continued Orla.

"And I think you should run along and build sandcastles or whatever it is twelve-year-olds do on holiday."

She was quite rude, thought Orla. "You're quite rude," she pointed out.

"You're quite annoying," replied the goth. "Don't come any further."

The girl ducked through a tunnel in the gorse and disappeared. Orla nodded at Dave, and then plunged into the burrow after her. It was a low and twisting passage, snaking through a miniature forest of thorny shrubs. Bent low, Orla didn't see the wire strung across the path. She tripped and fell, grazing her wrist on an exposed root. Tin cans dangling from the wire rattled an alarm, and there were more ahead. As Orla sucked her wound, Dave pushed past. Detecting booby traps was part of his job description. Treading carefully, the pair emerged in a little clearing protected by a thick roof of gorse and yet more tripwires hung with cans. The space was warm and dry, and dominated by a cheap blue dome tent.

"Cool camp," Orla said with a whistle. "Why all the security?"

The goth was unzipping the tent. Her muddy boots were standing beside a flat rock upon which lay a plastic lunchbox and an old penknife.

"Get lost," she said. "Go find someone your own age to hang out with."

Orla ignored the jibe. "Why do you think someone believes you're a witch?" she asked. "Apart from your weird dress sense?"

"You're funny," said the goth, but she wasn't laughing. She sat in the tent's porch and pulled off her wet socks. They had bats on them. "Can you go away, please?"

Dave sniffed the plastic lunchbox. Biscuits. Custard creams, probably a week old.

"And can you get that soggy mutt away from my stuff?"

There was a copy of *The Astronomical Almanac* on the floor of the tent.

"Are you a stargazer?" asked Orla.

The girl stared at her. "You're really annoying. Did I tell you that already?"

"Yes. But we need to talk."

"What makes you think I have the slightest interest in talking to a kid?"

Orla shrugged. "There's weird stuff happening here. I need to know why. I thought you might help."

"What weird stuff?"

Best not to mention the necklace, thought Orla. "A tree nearly fell on me," she said. "There aren't any birds except a crow. And I'm having really crazy dreams."

"That doesn't surprise me," muttered the goth. She looked at Orla. "Did the website mention that your charming holiday cottage is an old witch's house?"

"How do you know where I'm staying if you're not stalking me?" asked Orla suspiciously.

36

"It's my business to know who comes and goes," said the goth. She dragged a backpack from the tent, rummaged inside, pulled out a foil strip of tablets and popped two into her mouth. "Aspirin. You'll start getting the headaches soon too, and the nightmares will get worse," she said, taking a swig of water from a tin bottle. "It doesn't take long."

"There's no such thing as witches."

"You keep believing that, Nora, and you'll be fine."

"Orla," said Orla.

"Whatever. Look, I don't care if you believe it or not, but this place is bad for your health. People get sick. They have accidents. Weird ones. Cliffs collapse. Houses catch fire. Brakes fail on cars. Trees fall over. People die." She looked at Orla. "Lots of them."

"If you believe that, why are you here?" asked Orla.

The girl gazed at Orla from behind her fringe, as though trying to decide whether she could trust her or not. Then she sighed. "Because my dad was one of those who died and I want to find out why."

She gave Orla a slightly manic look, then shuffled into her tent and zipped it up. Her voice, slightly muffled, came from inside.

"You can go away now."

CHAPTER 5

"Nice walk, Orla the Explorer?" asked Richard, as his bedraggled sister dried Dave with the dog towel. He was lying on the sofa, staring at the ceiling like a prisoner contemplating a life sentence.

"Shh!" hissed Mum, head down in a pile of papers.

Orla gave Richard a serious look. "This place is extremely weird," she said quietly. "Where's Tom?"

At that moment, her little brother burst through the door. "There's a car coming down the lane," he cried breathlessly.

Mum didn't look up from her paperwork. "Probably lost tourists. Please don't throw anything at their car, Tom."

As Tom dashed back outside, a small beige car pulled into the clearing. Orla watched as the driver emerged balancing a cake tin and a bunch of flowers on her knee before slamming the door. She was in her late sixties, guessed Orla, and was dressed in a tartan skirt, black tights and green waxed jacket like a senior member of the Royal Family.

"It's a lady," she observed. "A proper one."

Mum dropped her Sharpie on the table. She threw her head back, groaned, then glanced urgently around the room.

"Richard – tidy that coffee table up."

From outside came a sudden outbreak of angry barking. Dave had just met the visitor. Tom came racing across the grass, yelling at Dave to shut the hell up and grabbing his collar. Dave kept barking, his fur spiked up and his fangs on show.

"Wow," exclaimed Orla. "Dave's acting really mental."

"Don't say mental," said Mum automatically. She wiped her hands on her skirt and opened the door. "Put that dog in the car right now," she yelled at Tom. Then she stepped outside to greet their visitor. "Hello. Sorry about him. Can I help you?"

Inside the car, Dave was still barking, fogging up the car window with his fury.

The lady was talking to Mum, but her gaze was focused through the kitchen window on Orla.

Oh God, thought Orla. It was the local detective. The most effective detectives were always old ladies. She'd come for the necklace.

The elderly sleuth came into the house, apologizing rather insincerely. "I'm so, so sorry to intrude but I wanted

39

to make sure the entire tribe had settled in." Her voice was more duchess than detective.

"Richard, Orla, this is Mrs Spark," said Mum. "She's the friend of Mrs Cottrall from church and she owns the cottage."

That didn't mean she wasn't a sleuth, thought Orla.

"Very pleased to meet you," said Richard, crossing the room to shake Mrs Spark's hand. He was good at social stuff. Orla, not so much. Suddenly overcome by shyness, she shuffled over and proffered her hand.

"Hello," she mumbled, in a rather weedy voice.

"What gorgeous red hair you have." Mrs Spark beamed.

It was a warm smile, thought Orla, but detectives were a cunning lot.

"Haven't a clue where she got it from," shrugged Mum.

"Mutant gene," said Richard.

"And who's the noisy little fellow outside?" asked Mrs Spark.

"That's Dave," said Orla. "He takes security matters very seriously."

"Well, I'll say hello to him later. Now look, chaps, I've brought offerings." She placed the bunch of flowers on the table. "Periwinkles and marigolds from my garden, and in here –" she pulled the top off the tin – "a freshly baked saffron cake. It's a local delicacy."

"How lovely!" enthused Mum. "You will stay and share it with us, won't you?"

"Golly," said Mrs Spark. "Are you sure I'm not imposing?"

She actually said "Golly". Orla bit her lip to stop herself laughing out loud.

Mum smiled. "Not in the slightest," she said. Orla let out a small, desperate sigh.

Tom put his head round the door, and Mrs Spark turned, extending her hand. "Hello, Dave," she said. "You're the security guard, I hear. Lucinda Spark. Lovely to meet you."

Tom frowned as Orla was struck by a fit of the giggles. "Dave's the dog. I'm Tom."

Once that small confusion was sorted out, the entire family sat down to eat saffron cake with Mrs Spark. It was all right, if a bit heavy on the currants.

"So, have you found out what's what in the neighbourhood?" asked Mrs Spark.

"Orla's been doing all the exploring," said Mum, topping up Mrs Spark's tea. "Tell Mrs Spark what you've found out, Orla."

Where to start? thought Orla. A fallen tree, an ancient treasure, a crow that flew through her dreams, a warning carved in sand and a weird goth hiding out on the clifftop.

She shrugged. "Not much."

"She said this place was – and I quote – 'extremely weird'." Richard grinned.

Orla threw him a furious look.

"Really?" said Mrs Spark. She didn't seem offended. "Do tell."

Fine, thought Orla, but if this was going to be an interrogation, she was going to be asking the questions.

"Who was Peter van der Mazie?" she asked.

Mrs Spark held her gaze. "I think you mean Pedervander Mazey, my dear."

"Oh," said Orla. "So who was he?"

Mrs Spark smiled. "He was a she, and she, if you believe what the locals say behind closed doors, was what you would call a witch. Where on earth did you hear that name?"

Orla went cold, then hot, then cold again. "I read it somewhere." It was a feeble response, and the look in Mrs Spark's eye proved she wasn't buying it for a minute. But, once again, she didn't seem offended.

"Honestly, Orla, there are so many stories around here of witches and devils and black dogs and ghost ships; and to be perfectly frank, most of them are made up just for tourists. But Pedervander Mazey, well, she was the real thing."

She kept her eyes on Orla just long enough for that to mean something, then glanced around the table. "Now then, has anyone been down to the beach yet?"

"We were going to take a look later, if the sun comes out," said Richard.

"Oh, it will." Mrs Spark nodded. "Any minute now, and the chances are you'll have the entire thing to yourselves. Except, of course, for the moryons on the coast path." She shot a glance at Tom. "That's the Cornish for outsiders, young man."

Tom's eyes widened. "Can you speak Cornish?"

Mrs Spark gave a modest little smile. "I've picked up a few words."

"What does Konnyck Vean mean?" asked Orla.

"It means 'cunning people'," said the old lady. "This cottage wasn't always called that, though. It used to be called Tregastenack, after the stream and the beach." Her eyes darted to the kitchen window. "See, chaps? As promised, the sun has come out." She drained her tea and stood up, brushing down her tartan skirt. "I'm going to leave you to your holiday."

Mum and Richard leapt to their feet. It was as though the Queen was in the parlour, thought Orla.

"Well, thank you so much for popping in," said Mum.

"Not at all," replied Mrs Spark. "Just thought I should introduce myself." She put a hand on the door, then turned to Orla.

"And if you, young lady, have any interest whatsoever in

local folklore, do pop round. I have a passion for the past and a lot of stories. I'm up at the old vicarage in the village, next door to the church. If Bessy's there, I'll be there too. Cheerio."

She strolled across the grass to her car, then turned and tapped the roof. "This, by the way, is Bessy. Oh, and the big rock in the bay is Gull Rock. Don't try and swim to it – it's a lot further than you think."

She waved as she drove away.

"She seemed quite nice," said Tom.

"I think she was just making sure that we were suitable guests," said Mum. "Tom – fetch my wellies please."

"I thought you were working?" said Richard.

"Not any more," replied Mum. "We're going to the beach."

CHAPTER 6

Richard stood on the shore in his worn-out wetsuit, his battered old board under one arm, searching for the rips. The sunshine promised by Mrs Spark had burned away the clouds and the sea had turned from sullen grey to a sparkling blue.

"You going to stand there all day?" asked Orla. She'd always loved swimming, but her long-awaited first dip of the holiday had been cut short by an inexplicable feeling of menace, as though the ocean meant her harm. There wasn't even a limpet, much less a crab, in any of the rock pools, and the weirdness was being made worse by Dave, who was spending the entire time barking at the sea. He didn't seem to be enjoying the holiday as much as Orla had hoped.

"You've got seaweed in your hair," observed Richard. "How cold is it out there?"

"Freezing," replied Orla.

She watched as her brother took a deep breath, threw

his board onto the white water and started paddling out through the breaking waves. He didn't make it look easy.

Keeping an eye on him – she couldn't shake that vague sense of impending doom – Orla pulled her shorts and T-shirt over her swimsuit and wandered along the high-water line, picking up the rubbish washed up by the tides. It never mattered how much she picked up, she thought, because the plastic just kept on coming.

She was stuffing a fistful of drinking straws and a plastic bottle from Argentina into her backpack when she spotted the goth girl. She was sitting on the big rock on the clifftop, her long black hair blowing in the wind. Her wrists flashed when her jewellery caught the sun, as though signalling something secret. She looked sad, thought Orla, as though she was thinking about her dad, or the mysterious force that had killed him. She wouldn't have mentioned it if she didn't want to talk about it, reasoned Orla, but, like Orla, she was probably wary about sharing too much with strangers. But there was a fix for that: she'd stop being a stranger and become the goth girl's friend.

* * *

"You again?" muttered the girl as Orla approached.

"Yep," smiled Orla.

The view was lovely in the sunshine. To the left, green

46

cliffs rolled all the way to a huge radio mast somewhere past Mevagissey. To the right, grey rock faces leapfrogged all the way to the Carrick Roads. In front, the sea looked like corrugated blue steel, and, in the far distance, a container ship was steaming to Falmouth.

"That your brother trying not to drown out there?" asked the goth.

"Yep," said Orla.

"Does he know he can't surf?"

"Nope."

Together they watched as Richard fought with the Atlantic swell. He'd fight to push through the breaking waves, getting pummelled and hurled back to shore by the white water. Eventually he'd make it to the rolling valleys behind, spend a few minutes catching his breath and then try to catch a wave, arms spinning like a Mississippi paddle steamer. Almost every time the wave rushed past, leaving him bobbing in its wake. When he did succeed, it was even worse. As his board was lifted by the surf, he raised himself into a wobbly press-up position and then sprang to his feet. And almost instantly, he fell off.

"Rinse and repeat," muttered the goth. She glanced at Orla. "What are you doing here?"

"Came to say hello."

"Hello."

"What's your name?" asked Orla.

The goth sighed and looked out to sea, where Richard was trying to remount his board, and to the beach, where Dave was running in tight circles.

"Why is your crazy dog barking at the sea?"

"I have no idea. He does lots of things no one really understands. So what did you say your name was?"

The goth ignored the question.

"Is it Vampyra?" asked Orla.

The older girl simply stared out to sea, so Orla climbed onto the rock and sat beside her, hugging her knees.

"Is it Elvira?" she guessed. "Or Drusilla, or Pantera?"

"God, you're irritating," sniffed the goth.

Orla nodded. "And persistent. It's Morticia, isn't it?"

She turned to look at Orla. "Can you please just go away?"

Orla shook her head. "Nope."

"Why not?"

"Because I know stuff. Stuff you should hear about."

The girl brushed dried mud from the hem of her dress, her bangles jingling. "Sure you do."

Orla traced a little circle on the rock with her finger. "I know all about Pedervander Mazey," she said.

The actual truth was, all she knew about Pedervander Mazey was that she had red hair, wore a green dress,

48

appeared in dreams but was a real person and a real witch. Tomorrow she would find out more, but just mentioning the name ought to be enough, she figured.

"Pedervander who?"

"Pedervander Mazey," repeated Orla. "She was a witch. That's what the locals say."

"What locals?"

"Mrs Spark who owns our cottage told me."

The girl gave Orla a deeply suspicious look, her eyes narrowed. "Are you one of them?"

"One of what?"

"The coven."

"What coven?"

The goth sighed in exasperation. "*The* coven."

"Oh," said Orla. "No. I'm Orla. I'm from London, and we've come to Cornwall for our holiday because we can't afford to go camping in France like I wanted to. And I haven't a clue what *the* coven is."

"They're witches," said the goth. "Their lord is Bucca Dhu and they're the custodians of evil. Every death that happens here is because of them."

Orla gave her a quizzical look. "Er, OK," she said slowly. "But this is the twenty-first century. Not the Dark Ages."

"You're fooling yourself. Everyone does, but you can't say you haven't felt it. You told me yourself that weird things have been happening. No birds here, you said, right?"

"Except a crow."

"Find any lobsters in the rock pools?"

"Nope."

"Exactly. And there's no phone signal, even though the biggest phone mast in the South West is just over there. No animals in the fields. Weird lights at night. Headaches. Sickness. And accidents. Too many accidents. It's witchcraft."

"Witchcraft?" echoed Orla, trying not to laugh.

The goth nodded. "Trust me. I've been studying this stuff for years. Witchcraft is alive and well in rural Britain."

"But have you ever actually spotted any witches around here?" asked Orla.

"Not so I could pick them out in an ID parade, but I've seen them. They light candles in the woods at night. They root around in the churchyards. And since they carved that message in the sand, I suspect they think I'm one of their kind."

"Are you?"

She shook her head. "Far from it." She leaned against the rock, and when she spoke again, her voice was quiet. "Do you know the book *Gobbolino*?"

"Yep." Orla nodded. *"Gobbolino the Witch's Cat."*

The girl nodded sadly. "My dad was a rescue diver in the navy. Ten years ago this month, he read me the whole of *Gobbolino*. Then he kissed me goodnight, left our house and disappeared from our lives. They found his body on Sidmouth beach two weeks later. The coroner's verdict was that he had drowned himself."

"That's awful," said Orla.

"The point is," continued the goth, "he'd spent the week before his death here. I didn't know that until recently – all the navy would tell us was that he'd been involved in a search and retrieval operation on the south Cornish coast."

"What's that got to do with witchcraft?" asked Orla. "I mean, it's really sad, but it could have been for any number of reasons."

"No, it couldn't. There were four men on his team. Two, including Dad, were dead the week after they came here. The third is in a secure psychiatric unit just outside Bristol. The fourth disappeared. The navy doesn't accept any responsibility for what happened and refuses to tell us anything other than what I've already told you."

She looked at Orla. "The one who disappeared was a guy called Graham Stokes. Took me a year to find out where he was. No email, no Facebook, no online presence whatsoever. Totally off-grid."

"So how did you find him?"

The goth shrugged. "Lucky, I guess. He'd joined a village library in Wales that hadn't updated its security software since 2008. My bot found his name on their database. I hacked it, got his address and wrote him a letter. Old style, with a stamp and stuff. Heard nothing, then last term I'm coming out of school and this creepy guy comes up to me."

"Graham Stokes?"

"Yep. He's got long greasy hair, bloodshot eyes, a nervous twitch and I can see he's freaking terrified. He says he can't help me. Just tells me to get on with my life and stop chasing ghosts. Then he says, 'Forget Poldevel.'"

Orla frowned. "And?"

"Until that moment I had never heard of Poldevel. The navy told my mum Dad had been working in Falmouth. So I did some digging. Found out that this coast – from Mevagissey in the east down to the Roseland in the west – is a total black spot when it comes to unexplained deaths. People die suddenly here, in weird and unexpected ways. They fall off cliffs. They get struck by lightning. Trampled by cows. Decapitated by barbed wire. Electrocuted by fallen cables." She glanced at Orla. "Crushed by trees. Nothing has been written about this. You won't find it in any books or newspapers. But the evidence is out there. Go look in the woods behind the churchyard. There's a mass grave there. 'Taken by the Devil' it says on the headstone."

She gave Orla a sideways look, her fringe falling across her eyes. "You need to experience this stuff for yourself. You need to *see* this coven. Feel the wickedness. Until then, Dora, you're just another dumb tourist."

"It's Orla," retorted Orla. "And I didn't catch *your* name."

A solitary crow glided overhead, carried on the salt breeze. The goth watched it pass and then turned to Orla. "My name is Raven."

CHAPTER 7

When the crow returned that night, Orla was ready. He led her up the side of the valley, through a blackthorn thicket and into open fields splashed silver by a gibbous moon. A left turn along a hawthorn hedge took her seawards. Beyond the cliff edge she could see the ocean glinting like mercury, and the warm air was sweet with honeysuckle. The crow swooped low and perched on a stone gatepost. He knew she didn't need him any more. A green flame was burning in the darkness, and Orla walked towards it.

"I watched you coming, girl."

The voice was female, the words mired in a thick Cornish accent. It sent a shiver through Orla that started between her shoulder blades and rippled to her knees. It's just a dream, she thought, chasing the fear away. Just a movie in your head. Enjoy it.

"You followed the sprowl path. It do take a bit longer that way, don't it?"

The flame flickered in and out of focus. Then it wasn't a

flame at all, but a girl, tall and lean, eighteen at most, her head covered with a shawl that shadowed her face. From beneath it, red hair fell in spirals across her shoulders and down her long green dress. Around her neck she wore a string of yellow beads that glowed faintly in the moonlight. Her skin was pale, her mouth wide, her slender fingers wrapped around a tall, forked stick upon which she leaned for support.

"You're Pedervander Mazey," said Orla.

The girl nodded. "I am," she said.

"This is just a dream, right?"

"It's more than that. You see me whole, but in truth I'm less than half of myself. I'm weak, child, and time is short."

She half turned into the moonlight, and Orla saw the stains on her dress. Splatters across the shoulders, and black from hip to thigh.

"You're hurt."

"I told you," said Pedervander. "But half of me remains." She pulled the shawl from her head, revealing a deep cut that began beside her right nostril, split her lips and ended on her chin.

"Oh my God," gasped Orla.

Pedervander smiled sadly. "There's nothing you can do, because neither of us is really here. These wounds never healed. You see me as I am before I die. As I told you, child, time is short."

The words came softly but the realization was like a door slammed in Orla's face. Slashed across the face and stabbed in the side, Pedervander was bleeding to death.

"We need to apply pressure to that wound," she said, reaching for the backpack that wasn't there. "We need to make a compress and—"

Pedervander grabbed her wrist in an icy grip. "I told you, girl: there's nothing you can do because I'm not here."

"So how can I see you?" spluttered Orla. "What does 'more than a dream' mean? Are you a ghost?"

"It's easier not to ask."

"You mean it's easier for you to avoid explaining," retorted Orla.

Pedervander looked at her, half a smile on her pale lips, as though approving of Orla's spirit.

"Have you seen a magic lantern?" she asked. "It uses glass and light to cast a picture onto a wall."

"We've moved on a bit since then," said Orla, "but I know what you're talking about."

"I am like one of those pictures, beamed not through space but through time in the hope that I would be seen."

"Who's operating the lantern?" asked Orla.

"I am," replied Pedervander. "It's a conjuration of the most powerful magic, and it tires me, girl."

"So why did you call me here?"

"Come," ordered Pedervander. "The serpent is kind in this light. I'll show you the compass." She turned and strode along the clifftop.

"Serpent?" asked Orla, jogging to catch up.

"I'm talking about Sarf Ruth," said Pedervander. "The sacred fire that slithers through the earth like a snake. You should know these things. You're a peller, girl."

"What's a peller?"

Anger flashed in Pedervander's eyes. "There's no time for childish games."

"I'm not playing," protested Orla. "Honestly. I'm from London. I'm just here on holiday."

"You're from London Town? Why so far?"

Orla shrugged. "It's where I go to school."

"School? I called for a peller, not a gentlewoman." She peered hard into Orla's face. "Who are you, girl?"

"Orla Perry."

Pedervander Mazey nodded sadly. "Stop here, Orla Perry, and close your eyes. Tell me what you feel."

Orla closed her eyes, and immediately felt a force – a humming vibration that seemed to rise and fall beneath her feet like the suck and the thump of the waves, a hundred metres below. Startled, she opened her eyes.

"The ground is shaking," she said. She looked around. They were standing near the middle of a wide circle of low boulders. "I can feel it throbbing. That's crazy."

"That's sprowl," said Pedervander.

"What's sprowl?"

"The earth's life force, girl. It rises here in great concentration, and on a night like this" – she nodded towards the moon – "it's benign. That you feel it is a blessing, but then you wouldn't have come if you weren't blessed with the cunning. You're going to need a gwelen."

"A what?"

"A staff of sacred wood," said Pedervander. "Like this one." She planted her stick in the ground and gripped it with both hands. "It'll store more sprowl than you can carry, but you can't go cutting any length of wood. Your staff will find you, and very soon." She threw Orla a sidelong glance. "I reckon you be willow or blackthorn, but we'll see."

"What are you talking about?" asked Orla. "Why am I here?"

Pedervander bit her lip. "I called for so many years, and it was you who came, but I fear you're not equal to the task." She closed her eyes, waiting for the pain to pass.

"What task?"

"To right the terrible wrong I have done."

"How?"

Pedervander looked as though it was only her stick that was keeping her upright. "You cannot ask, and I cannot tell," she said. "The deed must be conceived and performed by one pure of heart and devoid of rapacious intention. Those are the words of the Old One."

"The Old One?"

"The Horned One. Bucca Dhu. Lord of the Earth. It's he who guides us, but you must learn this for yourself, and there is much to learn."

"Like what?"

The peller shook her head. "There's no time left. Not now. If Bucca gives me the strength, we may meet again." She reached into the pocket of her dress and pulled out something small. "I'll leave this token for you," she said. "That way you'll know this was more than a dream."

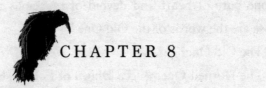

CHAPTER 8

Orla's eyes snapped open. Outside, a pale grey dawn. Inside, a framed picture of a cow with a dead fly trapped behind the glass and a threadbare rug on draughty floorboards. A tasselled lampshade and woodchip wallpaper. Very slowly, she swung her legs out of bed and, pulling her red hair away from her face, peered down at her feet.

No mud.

That had to be a good thing, right? Clean feet meant she hadn't actually followed a crow to the clifftop at midnight to meet with a copper-haired phantom with a bleeding wound. It was, after all, just a dream.

Orla took a deep breath, let her head thud back on the pillow, grabbed her old rag doll and closed her eyes.

"It was just a dream, Mala," she mumbled. "But you knew that already, right?"

The doll said nothing. Orla's eyes sprang open.

It was more than a dream.

Five minutes later, she was leading a yawning Jack

Russell out of the cottage and into the mist.

Dave had always believed that if you went out at dawn, you owned the day. Plus he liked to see the changeover as the night prowlers – the owls, the foxes and the badgers – holed up for the day and the day shift, chivvied along by the blackbirds, arrived to take their place.

But there were no blackbirds here, and not even a sniff of a badger. No life at all. No foxes, no rabbits, no voles and no squirrels. No pigeons or sparrows or gulls. Just the same old crow, flapping from tree to tree above their heads. Dave didn't mind crows. They were almost as smart as Jack Russells, but to see just one was, well, odd. He jogged to catch up with Orla as she climbed the valley side, pushing past her and leading her into the mist-wreathed fields at the top. He didn't have a clue what she was up to, but since it was Orla, he was prepared for trouble.

Unlike Dave, Orla knew exactly what she was doing. She was just a little confused as to why. She was either on the edge of an extraordinary, unforgettable and life-changing adventure, or she was going quietly insane and would spend the rest of her life locked up in a secure facility while Richard sipped tea at her bedside, nodding sadly and confiding to the nurses that he always knew it would end this way.

The only thing about the last two days that she knew was real was the necklace, but hadn't Pedervander Mazey said she'd leave something at the compass for her? Something that she'd promised would prove this was all more than a dream.

Suddenly, Dave made an about-turn and scarpered in the direction from which they'd just come. Orla called after him, but to no avail, and watched in growing despair as he vanished into the mist. He was a very mysterious beast, she thought, and she had just begun to go after him when he reappeared, accompanied by a short figure waving what appeared to be a war sword.

"Drat," she muttered.

Tom was looking extremely pleased with himself.

"I heard you creeping about," he panted, when he'd caught up. "You were as subtle as an elephant in a plaster cast. Then I tracked your footprints up that path back there. Too easy." He burst into a fit of wet coughs.

"Well done, Sherlock," said Orla. "Where did you get the stick?"

"Found it," said Tom. It was longer than he was tall. "It's for beating off cows," he added. "They're the most dangerous animal in Britain, you know. They kill thousands of people every year."

"Wild exaggeration," said Orla. They were approaching the gap in the hedge and she had an eye out for blue tits, yellowhammers, goldfinches – any living thing would do. "Does Mum know you're here?"

"Still snoring," said Tom. "So where are we going?"

Orla shrugged. "Exploring." She pointed into the wall of mist. "Over there somewhere. What's wrong with your voice?"

"Sore throat," said Tom. He was swinging his stick as Dave made desperate lunges to snatch it from him. "You know you're acting really weird, Orla, don't you? I mean, weirder than normal."

Orla didn't have an answer to that, so she quickened the pace. She'd just found a gap in a hedge she'd only seen in her dreams – in thick mist. Just like she'd known exactly how to get to Konnyck Vean the other night. How was that possible?

They reached the cliff edge and gazed down. The sea was dozing beneath a thick duvet of grey fog. Dave used the distraction to grab Tom's stick and the two fought a brief tug of war. Tom won, and they walked on towards the headland.

Pedervander had called it the compass and it was just as Orla had dreamed: a perfect circle of thirteen boulders, half hidden in the bracken. Yet if she really had been here last night with Pedervander Mazey, the bracken would be trampled, wouldn't it?

"What's this?" asked Tom.

"Looks like a fairy ring," replied Orla distractedly. She was scanning the rocks for the token left by the girl in the green dress, the object she had said would prove to Orla that this was more than a dream.

"Can you feel anything?" she asked.

"Like what?"

"Like a kind of vibration?"

Tom shook his head. "Nope. Can we go?"

"We just got here," said Orla, bending down to part the bracken around a quartz boulder. The energy was still there, thudding gently like an overcooked pan of popcorn.

"It's amazing," she whispered, staring at the rock.

"God, you're weird," sighed Tom. He wandered off as Orla continued her search for whatever it was the ghost had left.

Then something odd happened. Dave had managed to snatch the stick from Tom and was trying to run with it, looking like a short-legged lion trying to carry a whole giraffe. Both kids knew that Dave didn't play like normal dogs. He'd never respected the bit about bringing the item back so it could be thrown again, preferring to take it as far away as possible and drop it. Or, if he had the time and inclination, bury it. The parks of north London were rotten with old tennis balls and brand-new rubber toys buried by Dave.

But this time was different. He jogged towards Orla, stopped a metre from the edge of the circle, dropped the stick and barked.

Orla looked at the stick, then at Dave. "Forget it, dog," she said. "You've tricked me too many times before."

Tom dived in, grabbed the stick, and ran away. Dave followed him, but one minute later, he was back, the stick in his mouth and his eyes narrowed as though he were approaching a fire.

Orla didn't need this now. "Stop it, Dave," she growled. "I'm not playing with you."

Dave picked up the stick and ran around the circle, dropping it on the north side and barking. It was actually quite a fine stick, Orla observed: strong and stout and straight and ... suddenly she got it.

It was as Pedervander had predicted.

Her staff had found her.

But that wasn't what Pedervander had left behind, Orla was certain. Yes, one prediction from the dream appeared to have come true – in that a slightly dog-chewed stick had come to her – but she wanted to find the token. Whatever it was, it would be a link between dreams and reality, and proof that she wasn't going mad.

She kept searching until Tom announced that he was

definitely leaving right this very second. At least she had the staff.

"Can I keep this stick?" she asked Tom.

"It'll cost you."

"How much?"

"Two quid."

"Don't be ridiculous. It's a stick."

"So give it back."

"Fine, you meanie. I'll pay you later."

It was now a few minutes after seven and the mist was quickly burning off. The sun had hauled itself clear of the sea with a stubbornness that said nothing was going to get in its way today.

"Beach," said Tom. "All day, right?"

Orla nodded. "Right."

"No shops, no garden centres, no National Trust, right?"

"Right," said Orla again. But she had other plans.

CHAPTER 9

"Where the hell have you two been?" demanded Richard as the pair came back to Konnyck Vean. He was sitting at the kitchen table with a wad of toilet paper wedged up his right nostril.

"Out and about," said Tom vaguely. "You're bleeding."

"Really?" sighed Richard.

"What happened?" asked Orla.

"Nothing. Just a nosebleed."

Tom lunged for the orange juice carton. "The sun's out so we're spending the entire day at the beach," he declared.

Orla filled a glass with water. "I'm not coming," she said. "I have to go and see Mrs Spark."

"You what?" gasped Tom. He looked utterly betrayed. "Why?"

"Because I have to."

"No, you don't."

"I do. She invited me."

"But not today," he pleaded. "Why can't you wait until a grey day?"

"Because I want to go today."

"To study local folklore, right?" asked Richard. There was dried blood on his chin and a suspicious tone to his voice. Something was going on and it was irritating him that he didn't know what.

Orla looked at him. "Yes. To study local folklore."

Tom slumped at the table, distraught. "I can't believe you're going to leave me with Mum," he moaned. "She'll test lesson plans on me or something. And he's no fun," he added, nodding at Richard.

"Look," said Orla. "I'll go to Mrs Spark's after breakfast and join you in time for lunch, OK?"

"No, you won't," muttered Tom.

He was absolutely right.

Mum seemed delighted that Orla wanted to visit Mrs Spark.

"I'll drive you," she offered.

"I want to walk," argued Orla.

"But if I drive you it'll be safer and you can wear that nice summer dress."

Orla was horrified. "Oh no," she said, backing off and shaking her head. "No way."

"I've got a splitting headache and I'm in no mood to

argue with a twelve-year-old," said Mum. "You're not going out looking like that."

"And I am not wearing a dress," said Orla, folding her arms across her T-shirt. "Nope. No way. Absolutely not. And I'm walking."

An hour later she was sitting in the car wearing that nice summer dress and scowling like a pig on the way to market.

"Be polite to Mrs Spark, please," said Mum. "And don't forget please and thank you."

Orla grunted. She felt ridiculous.

"And leave that stupid stick in the car."

"But I like this stick," said Orla.

Mum stopped at the end of the muddy lane, waiting for a tractor to pass. "You are an odd girl, Orla Perry," she sighed.

They found the old vicarage quickly. It was right where Mrs Spark had said it would be, and Bessy was parked outside.

"I'll take you in," said Mum.

"Mum, I'll be fine."

Orla grabbed her stick, jumped out of the car, walked down a gravel path through a garden crowded with flowers, and knocked on the door. Wisteria flowers dangled from the vines covering the walls, dripping with dew like purple stalactites. Orla held her tongue out to catch a drop, then remembered that she was supposed to be behaving. She felt like an idiot in that stupid dress.

The door creaked open.

"Hello, Orla." Mrs Spark smiled.

"Morning!" cried Mum from somewhere behind. "I hope my daughter isn't interrupting anything, but she insisted on coming."

"Not at all," cried Mrs Spark. "It's lovely to have company. I'll drop her back a little later."

As Mum drove away, Mrs Spark placed a hand on Orla's shoulder. She was wearing an even more ridiculous dress than Orla – a strange, flowery, floaty thing accessorized with silver bangles and a selection of odd-looking necklaces. Her hair was hidden under a red bandana and her feet were bare. She was a very different Mrs Spark from the tweedy duchess who had brought the saffron cake. Her voice was still posh though.

"Come in," she said, pulling Orla by the hand. "I'm so glad you came." She paused, looking at the stick in Orla's hand like a blackbird examining a worm. "You can leave that on the step," she added.

The house was pretty much what Orla had expected: the clean yet cluttered home of an old lady who didn't mind being alone. China ornaments on shelves, clocks in corners and a hoard of framed photographs and old paintings on the walls. The place smelled of beeswax and lavender, and as she followed Mrs Spark down the long, tiled hallway, Orla decided that this was the kind of house she wanted when she was old.

"Have you had breakfast, dear?" asked Mrs Spark, leading the way into a big, bright kitchen dominated by a huge pine table. There were slate tiles on the floor, shelves full of glass jars, and the kind of log-burning cooker that Orla knew Mum would sell a child to own.

"Ages ago," said Orla. "Thank you."

An enormous iron key lay on the table.

"Cup of tea?"

"No, thank you," smiled Orla. "Could I have a glass of water, please?"

Mrs Spark beamed. "I'll make you something better."

She stood on tiptoes and lifted down a bottle filled with a red liquid. "Rosehip syrup," she said. She lifted down another bottle, darker. "And hawthorn syrup."

She took a carton of milk from the fridge. "That, in case you're wondering, is what proper keys used to look like."

"Can I touch it?"

"Of course you can," said Mrs Spark, pouring milk and syrup into a tall glass. "It's one of the only two keys for St Goran's Church down the lane."

"Where's the other one?" asked Orla.

Mrs Spark glanced theatrically around the room, then bent to whisper in her ear. "It's hidden by Captain Hemming's headstone. Only the church wardens are allowed to know that."

She handed Orla the glass. "Take your milkshake into the back garden and I'll join you in a jiffy."

CHAPTER 10

Mrs Spark's garden, bursting with leaf, tendril and bloom, was as magnificent to the nose as it was to the eye. Orla sniffed a drift of tall, pink flowers.

"Careful," warned Mrs Spark as she bustled into the garden. "That's valerian. The scent will make you drowsy." She grabbed a handful of green flowers from the pergola. "Mix valerian root with these hops and you've got as potent a knockout formula as anything a pharmacist can sell, but the difference is that this is safe. See this?" She caressed a spiky plant with purple flowers. "Comfrey. Best cure anywhere for scars. But you didn't come here today to talk about herbal remedies, did you?" She took a seat at a shiny wooden table and beckoned Orla to sit opposite. "I believe you wanted to talk about folklore."

"Tell me about Pedervander Mazey," said Orla. "Please." It was always best to get straight to the point, she thought.

Mrs Spark smiled. "Pedervander Mazey and her mother lived at Tregastenack Cottage for seven years from 1805.

That's when the locals changed the name to Konnyck Vean, which means 'cunning folk'."

So Orla really was on holiday in a witch's house – just as Raven had said.

"And Pedervander Mazey was an actual witch?" asked Orla, careful not to let her face betray her beating heart.

"She was, but the correct term is 'peller'. It's an old Cornish word for one who repels."

"Repels what?"

"Repels those things that other people don't want in their lives."

"Like what?"

"Like aches and pains, for example."

"Like a doctor, then?"

"More than that. A peller can turn away bad weather, sickness in animals, evil intentions. Some can even bring people back to life. Basic first aid, in all likelihood, but back in Pedervander Mazey's day breathing life into a drowned child was miraculous."

She brushed a dead moth from the table. "But a peller doesn't only repel. A peller can make things happen – good or bad. A peller can make you fall in love and then, just like that, she can break your heart. She can banish dark spirits, or send them to your door." Mrs Spark looked up at the sky, its blueness broken only by the white track of a westbound jet. "A peller can bring warm sunshine, or ferocious storms, and she has the otherworldly folk at her beck and call: piskies, knockers, spirions and the like. Have you heard of these?"

"Pixies, yes, but—"

"Not pixies. Piskies – the spirits of the dead. Knockers are spirits of the mines, and spirions are not nice at all. They're all out there, but only the pellers know where."

Orla's leg was trembling. She hoped Mrs Spark hadn't noticed.

"Was Pedervander good or evil?" she asked.

"Now that depends who you ask. I think it's fair to say she started out trying to be good, but ended up being very, very bad. A lot of folk will tell you she was as evil as evil can be. Others say she was a misunderstood child who acted out of blind grief to avenge a terrible crime."

Behind Mrs Spark, hanging from the eaves of a wooden outbuilding, something that looked an awful lot like a dog's spine was dangling from a rusty chain.

"Why blind grief?" asked Orla.

Mrs Spark flicked something from her sleeve. "Heartbreak, my dear. She fell in love with a local criminal called Cadan Leverick and, as criminals are wont to do, he betrayed her."

"What kind of criminal?"

Mrs Spark drummed her fingers on the table, as though irritated by the question. "Cadan was the son of Blyth Leverick. Blyth was the leader of the Carne Gang: a particularly nasty mob of local pirates."

Orla blinked hard and thought very carefully about what she'd just heard. "So you're telling me that a beautiful witch fell in love with a handsome pirate who broke her heart? Seriously?"

Mrs Spark laughed. "I knew you'd find it hopelessly romantic, but I never said she was beautiful nor that he was handsome. For all we know she was a toothless hag and he was a one-eyed hunchback. There's no one living who can say otherwise."

She *was* beautiful, thought Orla. Or had been. She knew. She'd seen her.

"How did he betray her?" she asked.

"He made a deal with the local authorities. Tried to trade her life for his, the miserable dog. His plan didn't work, but the betrayal had terrible consequences, Orla. The Mazey girl had a temper, and she didn't forgive easily. She cursed every living thing in this parish. Not just the folk, but the livestock, the birds and the beasts, even the trees. She poisoned the earth and the sky and the waters with a curse so potent that it's taken an army of pellers to keep it at bay every single day since."

"A terrible wrong," mumbled Orla. That was what Pedervander had said up on the cliff.

Mrs Spark gave her a curious look. "A terrible wrong indeed."

"Is that why there's no wildlife?"

Mrs Spark nodded. "Well spotted."

Orla leaned forward, like a detective. "Are you one of them?"

Mrs Spark held her gaze. "I am."

"So you're a witch?"

"We really prefer the term 'peller', dear."

Orla's mouth stayed closed, but her eyes were saying OMG.

"There's no need to worry." Mrs Spark smiled. "We're quite normal, and our cause is a good one."

"Because you're trying to save the earth?" asked Orla.

"Well, we're having enough trouble trying to save this little bit of Cornwall," admitted Mrs Spark, "but ultimately, yes, because if we can't stop it this pollution of evil could contaminate the entire planet." She placed her hands on the table and leaned closer. "I'm deadly serious about this, my dear."

Orla put her hands on her head, as if that would stop it spinning. The morning was getting weirder and weirder.

"How did Pedervander spread this curse?" she asked.

"By using powerful, ancient magic. Magic she should never have been capable of. Until then the most remarkable thing she'd done was probably curing a lame cow, for goodness' sake."

"Why didn't people just move away?" wondered Orla. It seemed like an obvious question.

"Those who could, did. But this isn't just a matter of self-preservation, my dear. As I've said, there's a much bigger problem to deal with here. The coven isn't simply trying to keep the curse at bay. We're trying to contain it, because the further it spreads, the stronger it gets. The girl poisoned the very sprowl of the earth."

Sprowl. Sarf Ruth. Bucca Dhu. The earth's life force.

Orla looked hard into Mrs Spark's eyes. "Do you actually believe in all this?"

Mrs Spark held her gaze. "Yes, I do. And there are billions of decent people on this earth who believe that if they lead a good and pure life, they'll go to heaven when they die. Would you tell them their faith was rubbish?"

"People have totally misunderstood eternal life," said Orla.

Mrs Spark raised an eyebrow. "Oh, have they?"

"Yep. We're worm food when we die. The nutrients in our bodies nourish the trees. That's how life continues."

"You're very certain, aren't you? But try this." She tore

a bunch of hop heads from one of the stems she'd picked and placed them on the table. "Imagine each of these five green buds is a different world…"

"Four," corrected Orla.

"Five," insisted Mrs Spark.

"I can only see four."

"And I'm telling you there are five," said Mrs Spark, lifting one of the hop heads up to reveal another lying beneath it.

"Just because you can't see it, doesn't mean it doesn't exist. It can be light years away, or right alongside you. Maybe you catch a glimpse of it every now and then, but your hard-headed rationalism denies its existence. It's the other world – the supernatural, if you like."

Orla shrugged. "I understand the theory but I don't believe in it."

"Nor should you deny the possibility of its existence." Mrs Spark reached across the table and gripped Orla's hand. "I have seen the proof, Orla, and I know that this other world is very real indeed."

Orla pulled her hand away. Mrs Spark was happily heading off on a weird tangent and she didn't have time for that. She needed to steer the old lady back to the story.

"So what happened to Pedervander Mazey?"

Mrs Spark shrugged. "No one really knows. She was

wreaking havoc across a dozen parishes. People had died, and folk were scared to approach her. The only one to take her to task was the new vicar here in Poldevel – a brave chap called Jasper Bates. The story goes that he put the fear of God into her and she left Cornwall. Probably for Brittany." Mrs Spark stared into the space between her and Orla, as though she had a private window into the distant past. "It didn't stop the bad things happening, though."

Despite the warm sunshine, Orla was suddenly cold.

"What bad things?"

Mrs Spark took a deep breath. "Well," she said, "there had already been the shipwreck off Tregastenack beach. Seven of the victims are buried in the Old Ground. It's behind the graveyard. The rest were never found."

Tom had dreamed of a shipwreck. Raven had mentioned a mass grave. Orla felt goose pimples on her arms.

" 'Taken by the Devil'," she murmured.

Mrs Spark sniffed. "Quite the explorer, aren't you? But do you know why they're buried there?"

Orla shrugged.

"The Old Ground is where the pellers are buried. And their victims. Too risky, you see, to bury the cursed in consecrated ground."

"Maybe it was just an accident," argued Orla.

"Then explain this," said Mrs Spark. "Soon after the Mazey girl vanished in 1812, this place – the old vicarage – burned down, with poor, brave Reverend Bates inside. They said a candle had caught the curtains but..." She shrugged.

"There were more shipwrecks that winter, and the next, and the weather went from bad to worse. Folk started dying in terrible accidents: thrown from horses, hit by falling branches, trampled by cows..." Mrs Spark shook her head in exasperation. "You've seen the Lightning Shelter?"

Orla shook her head. Mrs Spark sniffed.

"It's a Stone Age rock tomb up on the cliff path above Tregastenack beach. It was excavated in 1818 so travellers could hide in it from the storms she sent. Lightning killed a lot of folk around here, but Mazey had other tools. In 1916, every man in Poldevel and Tremarra over the age of eighteen went to France or joined the navy. All twenty-two of them were killed, one way or another. They were the only villages in Britain that lost every man they sent, but it was hushed up so as not to hurt morale. Then there's the fishing trade. All but gone due to the number of boats that have gone down; and don't get me started on the problems the farmers have had. Diseased stock, plagues of rats, failed crops year after year."

81

"Why can't your witch army stop it?" asked Orla.

"I prefer to think of us as a sisterhood of like-minded environmentalists," said Mrs Spark sharply.

"Sorry," said Orla.

"We can't stop it because most of us are dead," said Mrs Spark. "Pedervander Mazey is killing us, one by one, and we can't stop her."

A cool breeze drifted through the garden like a ghost. The dog's spine tinkled, echoed by the faint ringing of the front doorbell.

Mrs Spark frowned. "Will you excuse me for a moment?"

As she wafted into the house, Orla threw back her head and let out a long groan. What on earth had she got herself into? She glanced around the garden, taking in the honeysuckle and the valerian and the pinks and the sweet peas and all those roses. It all looked so perfect, and if it hadn't been for that chain of red rocks under her mattress and her dreams of the girl in green, she would have been convinced that Mrs Spark was quite insane. She threw a disapproving glance at the bones dangling from the garden shed like a voodoo mobile. And it wasn't the only example of ghoulish garden decor: there were chains of femurs, ribs and skulls hanging over the back door and over every window, partly hidden by the wisteria. Orla brushed the bones hanging over the back door. They rattled like cheap wind chimes, the skull swinging around to glare at her from sightless sockets. Orla glared back. Old bones didn't scare her.

Mrs Spark bustled back into the garden, followed by an even older lady gripping a forked walking stick like a sparrow clasping a branch.

"I'm so sorry, Orla dear," said Mrs Spark, "but there's been an incident."

The old lady gave Orla a thin, apologetic smile.

"Mrs Perran, meet Miss Orla Perry. She's staying at Konnyck Vean." She beckoned Orla closer. "My dear, this is Mrs Perran. She could tell you a few things about that Pedervander Mazey, but we don't have the time today."

Mrs Perran offered Orla a hand that was more bone than skin. "I'm so sorry to have interrupted, young lady," she said. Her voice was high-pitched and quavering, like a piccolo played in an abandoned church.

"Poor thing's broken her glasses," sighed Mrs Spark. "So I'm giving her a lift to Specsavers in Truro. Can we finish this another time? Tomorrow, maybe?"

"Yes, of course." Orla nodded.

"We'll drop you back at Konnyck Vean on our way," said Mrs Spark. "Unless, of course, you'd like to do some more exploring?"

"I'll explore," nodded Orla.

"Good girl." Mrs Spark pointed across the fields. "The prettiest way is along the stream. Don't get lost."

Mrs Perran gave Orla a very strange look. Maybe it was because her glasses were broken and she couldn't see. Or perhaps it was because she could see something very clearly indeed.

"Be sure to stick to the right path, girl," she said.

CHAPTER 11

Dragging her stick, Orla ambled along beside the stream, happy to let the water lead her home. Normally she would have been on the lookout for kingfishers, water voles and otters, but what was the point? Mrs Spark had confirmed that there was no wildlife, and, frankly, her mind was too busy to focus. It buzzed like a kicked hive, the thoughts circling like furious bees. She wished Mrs Spark had told her more, but she was also scared that the old lady had been learning as much about Orla as Orla had learned about Pedervander Mazey. And there was something odd about Mrs Perran. She had looked at Orla as though studying an exotic and possibly dangerous animal rather than a girl on holiday.

The stream flowed through a field and then into a circular wood of peeling silver birch and rough-barked oak. A sea of stinging nettles swayed on either side of the water, pricking her bare legs as she tiptoed through, but that didn't make this place cursed earth. Surely cursed earth was bitter, black and barren, with pools of toxic waste and the shrivelled stumps of poisoned trees. This place, on the other hand, was so green, so peaceful...

The snap of a breaking twig ended the tranquillity. Orla froze, the hairs on the back of her neck rising up like Dave's did when he felt a threat. She was far from home, deep in a wood and all alone.

But not quite.

Someone else was out there. Someone who was deliberately moving as quietly as possible. Orla turned in a slow circle, peering through the trees, wishing, once again, that she had Dave with her.

"Hello," she called. "Anyone there?"

Nothing stirred in the wood for three long minutes. Then as Orla turned, three footsteps crunched across the leaf litter.

She spun round, ducking low into the stream bed, moving fast upstream towards the sound. Whoever was stalking her would be looking where she had disappeared, not where she popped up, and that would buy her some time.

She stuck her head above the nettles just in time to see a black-clad figure vanish behind a tree.

"Raven?" she called out. "Is that you?"

The stalker didn't reply, but, whoever it was, they'd picked the wrong prey. Orla had studied and practised invisibility for as long as she could remember. It was quite easy when you knew how. Friends and family had long realized that games of hide-and-seek with Orla Perry quickly turned into a missing persons' inquiry. She ducked down again.

Far above, the noonday sun slid behind a cloud, and a cold shadow fell across the wood. There was a pungent smell in the air – like fresh blood and burnt iron – and Orla's hands were tingling from the nettle stings. But she remained absolutely still, like a leopardess stalked by a hunter.

Annoyingly, the hunter was just as patient, and now mist was drifting through the wood.

Not mist.

Smoke.

A sudden screech tore through the silence. It came from behind, followed by the hissing suck of something very dangerous moving fast and straight.

Time to move.

Staying low, Orla pushed a few yards upstream just as a vortex ripped through the nettles and across the water, leaving whirling plumes of smoke and steam in its wake.

Now, thought Orla, was probably a reasonable time to be scared. She'd only caught a glimpse and it was black.

Just black, liquid darkness.

It sparked a terror Orla had never felt before and one that she wasn't sure she could control.

Another squeal echoed through the wood, and as Orla stuck her head further above the nettles she saw a whirlwind of nothingness tearing a path through the trees straight towards her.

It was time to run.

Downstream.

Up the bank.

Behind that rock.

The darkness scorched past, like Death on his mare, and Orla knew that if she stayed still, it would find her, so she ran again.

Through the trees, beside the stream, zigzagging, aiming for the light at the edge of the wood, feeling the sting of ripped leaves and splintered twigs against the back of her legs, diving left behind an oak as the darkness ripped past again.

Somehow she knew that if she could get out of the wood she'd be safe. So she kept running. The stream re-entered the meadow maybe thirteen trees away.

She tripped at the ninth, skinning her knees and her hands. From somewhere behind her, a tree fell with a crack and a gasp as she rolled back to her feet and burst from the wood, running deep into the meadow.

Would it follow?

Orla spun round, her staff held in both hands like a war sword.

The darkness remained in the trees, flooding the wood like liquid tar, and from behind it, an old woman appeared. Black dress. Grey shawl covering her head and a smoking steel bucket in her right hand. Paying no attention to Orla, she tipped the bucket's contents into the stream.

With a hiss, the blackness vanished, and the woman turned to Orla. Her face was still hidden, but there was a flash at her throat – a silver star.

"The next time," she growled, "you'll perish."

"Who are you?" yelled Orla. "Why are you doing this?" But the figure simply turned and disappeared into the wood.

CHAPTER 12

"WHAT THE HELL HAPPENED TO YOU, ORLA PERRY?" bellowed Mum.

Orla held up her hands. "I got a bit lost," she said.

"That's always your excuse! I was just about to call the police."

Maybe she wouldn't notice the dress, thought Orla.

"And you've ruined that dress," shrieked Mum. "And your shoes. You see? This is why we can't have nice things." She dropped her voice to a whisper, and Orla knew what was coming next. "You're grounded, young lady. Get up those stairs and run yourself a bath. Then you stay in your room until dinner time. Understood?"

Orla nodded contritely, and trudged upstairs. Tom was in bed, playing on his Switch. Dave was at his feet, on his back, legs in the air, tongue hanging out and fast asleep.

"Hello, Tom."

"Go away," muttered Tom without looking up. "You

promised you'd come to the beach and save me and you didn't."

"Sorry," she mumbled.

"Mum spent the whole morning working, Richard was hanging out with some weird zombie and Dave and I just mooched about. I wasn't even allowed to go in the sea."

The weird zombie had to be Raven, thought Orla. Unless there were two weird zombies in the district.

"I said I was sorry," she said.

"Yeah, well, sorry's not good enough. Now you'll never know what Dave and I found because we're never going to tell you."

"Oh," said Orla in a small voice. "Hello, dog."

Dave opened one eye and studied Orla. There was something different about her – a dark, worrying aura – and he didn't like it. He jumped off the bed before Orla could touch him and hid underneath.

"Nice," she sighed. She tapped Tom's leg. "Why are you in bed?"

"Threw up. Mum says I have a temperature. Feel like crap. Great holiday we're having."

Orla, feeling awful, turned to go. Then she spotted the green stone on Tom's bedside table. It was perfectly round, the size of a cherry tomato, and encircled with a narrow band of crystal.

"That's amazing," she breathed. "Is this what you found?"

"Nope," said Tom. "That's a minor discovery. I found something much more interesting, but now you'll never know."

Orla reached for the stone.

"Leave it," he warned.

"Just looking. Where did you get it?"

"At that fairy ring thing we went to this morning. It was just lying there."

It was the token Pedervander Mazey had left. No doubt at all. "Can I have it?" asked Orla.

"Nope," said Tom.

"Please?"

"Nope."

"I'll buy it from you."

"You still owe me two quid for the stick."

"Yeah, I know. I'll give you another pound for the stone."

Tom looked up from his Switch, noticing Orla's be-draggled appearance for the first time. "What the hell happened to you?"

"Got a bit lost. So, a pound then?"

"A pound? No way. Twenty pounds."

Orla gave Tom her sad, orphan look. "I haven't got twenty pounds."

He shrugged. "That's your problem. Put my stone down."

"I'll do ten jobs for you."

"Like what?"

"Cleaning shoes, tidying your room, doing your chores. Anything."

"Wow," he said. "Why do you want it so much?"

"It's pretty."

"So let's say twenty jobs plus twenty pounds when we get back from holiday."

"That's robbery!" protested Orla.

Tom stuck his bottom lip out. "You don't have to buy it."

Orla sighed. "Fine." She pocketed the stone and went to run her bath.

Later, when only Malasana was watching, Orla thrust her hand under her mattress and pulled out the carrier bag. The necklace was coiled inside, its stones the colour of blood, the grime on its clasps like scabs. Orla knelt on the bedside rug, staring into the bag and feeling sick. The jewels and the dreams and Pedervander Mazey and Raven and the curse and whatever that was in the wood today were all connected. They had to be. But how? It was like trying to guess the picture on a thousand-piece jigsaw puzzle when you only had five of those pieces and three of them had been chewed by the dog.

She heard Mum's voice outside the room. "Orla? Can I come in?"

Orla shoved the bag back under the mattress. Mum's flip-flopped feet appeared on the bedside rug.

"What are you doing on your knees?" she said.

"Trying to work out what happened," replied Orla.

"Today, you mean?" asked Mum, sitting on the bed.

"No. Ever since we got here," sighed Orla, flopping down beside her.

Mum gave her a concerned look. "For such a clever girl, you always seem to be getting lost. Is that what really happened?" She placed a hand on Orla's arm. "Tell me, love, because I can help."

Orla let the day play back in her mind, 128x fast-forward. Mrs Spark. The curse. A snapped twig. Smoke, the squeals, the darkness. The woman with the silver star and the ashes tipped into the stream.

She looked up at Mum. Mum definitely wouldn't be able to help.

"Not really," she said.

"What do you mean, 'not really'? Did anybody…" She paused. "Did anybody try and hurt you?"

Orla looked her mother in the eye. "No," she said. "Mrs Spark had to take Mrs Perran to Specsavers and she said she'd drop me home but I wanted to walk."

"Yes," said Mum slowly. "And then what happened?"

"I told you. I followed the stream looking for wildlife but got lost." She felt her cheeks burning. Mum was right: that excuse was getting a bit tired. "And I'm sorry I messed up my clothes."

"Again," added Mum. She shook her head. "Don't worry. The dress can be repaired and you can clean the shoes. But I'm furious with that silly old woman for letting you go wandering off. She should have brought you home like she promised, regardless of what you wanted."

"I wanted to explore," said Orla.

"No excuse," said Mum. She cast a critical eye over her daughter. "And you shouldn't wear odd socks."

Orla looked down. One was bright red, the other black and white stripes. "Can't find the other striped one."

Mum sighed. "It's either in your bag, or in the drawer. But listen to me, Orla. You're not from around here. You're a city kid. There are things out there that people like us don't understand."

Orla nodded. There was more truth in that than Mum realized.

CHAPTER 13

Dinner, when it came, was average: pasta and sauce with frozen garlic bread.

"What happened to you?" grunted Richard, giving Orla a sidelong stare of undisguised suspicion. "You look like you've seen a ghost."

Much worse than a ghost, thought Orla. She blinked hard, slapped a nonchalant smile across her face and reminded herself not to give the game away.

"Nothing much." She shrugged. Time to change the subject. "How was the surf?"

"He didn't go surfing," said Tom. "Too busy talking to his girlfriend."

"She's not my girlfriend."

"That's not what it looked like to me," retorted Tom.

"Hey," said Mum. "Be nice to each other."

"That's exactly what Richard and his girlfriend were doing," said Tom, sniggering.

"Really?" said Orla.

"Er, no, actually," said Richard, blushing. "We were just talking – not that it's any of your business."

"They were talking about phone signals," reported Tom. "She can't get one either. But she saved a wasp."

"She did what?" asked Mum, taking a slurp of wine.

"Saved a wasp. It was drowning in a rock pool and she fished it out. Dave ate it."

"Lovely," said Mum. "What's she like, Richard?"

Richard gave his mother a look of exasperation, "What do you mean 'what's she like'?"

Mum chewed her pasta thoughtfully. "You know: is she clever, arty, funny? She's clearly kind to animals."

"Wasps aren't animals," said Tom.

"She's a bit strange, to be frank," conceded Richard. "She thinks this place is evil. Which was exactly the same conclusion you reached, was it not, dear sister?"

Orla took a sip of water. "I never said it was evil. It is a bit weird, though. But I thought that before I met Raven."

Three pairs of eyes skewered her.

"Who's Raven?" asked Richard.

"Your girlfriend," said Orla. "Didn't she introduce herself?"

"She's not my girlfriend," sniffed Richard. "She's way too alternative for that."

"Whatever." Orla shrugged. "Anyway, I met her yesterday morning."

"Where's she staying?" asked Mum.

"Dunno," lied Orla. There was no need for Mum to know that Raven was camped in a gorse copse surrounded by tripwires and alarms to keep the witches away.

"At a caravan park." Richard sighed. "Any further questions?"

"I'm just interested," said Mum, refilling her glass. "What do her folks do?"

"I have no idea," said Richard. "She said her dad was in the navy but he died ten years ago."

"That's sad," said Tom.

"People die all the time," said Orla.

"In mysterious circumstances," continued Richard. "She thinks the answer might be here." He reached across to grab the last piece of garlic bread. "But then she's very weird. Like Orla."

"Your sister is not weird," said Mum. "She's just different."

"Thanks for that," muttered Orla.

Sometime in the darkness between midnight and sunrise, the crow came again.

Orla followed him up the valley and across rain-swept

fields to the cliff. In the darkness below, the Atlantic was dashing the rocks with violent thumps and whiplash hisses, and the salty wind was trying to blow Orla away. At last the path began to descend, following a hawthorn hedge that crackled with that earthly energy Pedervander Mazey called sprowl. Darkened houses and a church tower emerged from the gloom.

Orla climbed a stile beside a nettle bed and found herself on a steep cobbled street. Cottages leaned in from both sides, spilling no light. The crow called, and Orla followed, down to where the waves smashed against the harbour wall. She heard voices – the harsh cackles of drunken men – and then she saw the candle glow: a dirty yellow pool on the wet cobbles. The wooden sign swinging above the door said *The Magpie*, and when the crow perched on it Orla understood. She was supposed to go inside.

The place smelled of alcohol, sweat and strong tobacco, and Mum would have had kittens if she'd known where Orla was. Sticking to the shadows, she crept up to a window and, standing on tiptoe, peered inside. The glass was rain-streaked and dirty, but she could make out four figures sitting around a table, their heads close, their voices low. Yells and guffaws were coming from another room in the tavern, but these men were clearly talking business.

Suddenly, a rough hand was clamped around her mouth

and she was dragged away. She bit down hard, tasting dirt and blood, and hacked her captor's shins with her heels. He gasped, and threw her to the ground.

"Demon," he hissed, swiping at her hair.

Orla wriggled out of reach, turned and climbed to her feet, only to be knocked flat again, her legs swept from beneath her by a booted foot. She turned to face him, her hand closing around her staff as her attacker pulled a knife from his belt.

"Wanna die tired, do ye?" he said, taking a step closer.

"It'll be you who perishes, Abram Penburthy," said a second voice.

Orla's attacker backed off, his eyes wide in terror.

The voice belonged to Pedervander Mazey. She held out her hand to Orla. "Get up and come with me."

Feeling very small yet highly visible, Orla followed Pedervander Mazey into the tavern. All eyes were on a man swinging a ball on a string into a clay cup, shouting out the numbers as his score rose, and no one saw them pass. They opened a door into another room. The four men Orla had seen through the window were in there, with two black dogs, their yellow eyes flashing in the candlelight.

"I'm back," announced Pedervander, leading Orla to a bench under the window. The dogs slid apart to make space.

"God help us," muttered one of the men.

"God won't save you from that devil," grinned another.

A third man slammed his tankard down on the table. "You watch your mouth, you damn fool," he growled. "We need blessings not curses." He turned to Pedervander. "I'm sorry for this fool's mouth, Miss Mazey."

Orla sat on the bench next to the peller. "What's happening?" she whispered.

Pedervander kept her eyes on the men. "There's no need to whisper," she said. "They can't see you and they can't hear you, because you're not here." She swung her gaze to Orla. "Truth be told, I'm not here either. I was, when this happened, but I'm at my hearth now, reliving what took place this night with you. It's complicated, child."

"I don't understand," admitted Orla.

"Perhaps you should," sighed Pedervander. "What you see and hear this night and others is through the window of my memory."

"I still don't get it," said Orla. "Am I here, or in bed? Is this a dream or reality?"

The peller rubbed her eyes in exasperation. "It's more than a dream and less than reality. As I told you: I'm at my hearth. And you're probably in your bed. We have met across the decades ..."

"The centuries," interrupted Orla.

"Centuries?" gasped Pedervander. "I cast my memories

101

across centuries and you caught them. It's as though I threw a rock over the curve of the sea and kin beyond the horizon snatched it from the sky." She blinked away her surprise. "They said such magic is beyond the means of mortals and yet I see you, and you see me."

"I agree that it's freaky," nodded Orla. "But what about the man outside?"

Pedervander nodded. "A conjuring as powerful as this casts a shadow across the spirit world, and those with second sight will see it. Old Abram is one of them, but there's none here who believe a word he says."

Orla stretched to stroke the dogs. They were lying at her feet and yet she couldn't reach.

"You can't touch them," said Pedervander. "They're Wisht Hounds. A conjuring for protection. They exist only in the mind. Unlike them." She nodded at the men. "Him with the red face is Bloody Blyth Leverick, and them others is mostly his men. They're pirates, and since Jesus won't help them, they pay me to bless their wicked endeavours with spells and charms."

She looked at Orla, her eyes cloudy as sea glass. "On the high tide, they set sail for the Carib. This night is where the evil begins. For the sake of some pretty stones, all here will die."

"The necklace," said Orla.

Pedervander nodded. "Yes, girl."

"I found it in a tree," revealed Orla.

"I know. I put it there before the men came for me."

"What should I do with it?"

"Don't let it lie near them that aren't blessed by Bucca. It will kill them like slow poison. Take it to a sacred place and hide it well."

"And then what?"

"I can't tell you, and nor must you ask. The decision must be yours alone. A choice conceived and performed by one pure of heart and devoid of rapacious intention, remember?" She glanced at a stub of candle, spluttering in a clay saucer. "I'm weak now. We have until the light burns out." She looked Orla in the eye. "There'll be no more dreaming hereafter."

Orla looked at Pedervander's hands, the fists clenched like a crow's talons; at the cut across her face and at the black blood stiff on her green dress.

"Who did this to you?" she asked.

"Men like these. They haven't done it yet but a bad night is coming, and when it does I'll hurt this village, and the next one, and the next, as far as Penzance and beyond, God help me."

Orla reached out and touched the peller's sleeve, feeling the coarseness of the fabric.

"You don't have to hurt anybody, Pedervander," she said.

The girl in green snatched her arm away. "Don't be a fool," she hissed. "I will be betrayed for those fine jewels and in vengeance I will kill my betrayers and curse their kin until kingdom come." She looked at Orla, her eyes wet with tears. "But it will be a mistake. A terrible mistake that I cannot put right." She lowered her head, as though praying. "Until the next full moon…"

This wasn't the story Mrs Spark had told. She'd mentioned betrayal, yes, but nothing about fine jewels. An outbreak of cheering from outside the room interrupted Orla's thoughts.

"What's happening?" asked Orla.

The door flew open, and a tall man wearing a rain-soaked watch coat and high boots strode into the room. His hair hung in wet black streaks across his face and as he smiled at Pedervander his eyes glowed as green as her dress.

Pedervander lifted her chin. "He is what's happening," she said.

Cadan Leverick slammed the door and the candle sputtered out.

CHAPTER 14

It was light when Orla woke. She opened her eyes then closed them again. Bad idea – the shards of last night hit her like the splinters of a broken bottle.

A fight outside a pub. A conversation with a dead witch. The horror she'd felt when the candle went out, and the iciness of the rain running down her neck as she'd desperately dug a hole beside the fallen oak. Crazy dream.

Her eyes sprang open again. Her fingernails were clogged with Cornish earth. She frowned, then leapt out of bed and reached under the mattress. The carrier bag was gone. She whirled around, looking for Malasana. The doll too was gone.

So the last part wasn't a dream. She really had taken the necklace into the wood in the pouring rain in the dead of night, buried it in a hole and left Malasana to guard it.

She flopped back onto the bed and stared at the ceiling.

Was this what insanity felt like?

The door burst open and Tom stormed in like the police. "What happened to you?" he croaked.

"Bit of privacy would be nice," muttered Orla, hastily stuffing her muddy hands under the covers.

"Whatever. You're summoned."

"What time is it?"

"Gone ten."

"Ten?" gasped Orla. She never slept until ten.

"Richard's gone surfing and Mum's supposed to be taking me to the monkey sanctuary."

"Well, we'll all miss you, but I think you'll be much happier there," said Orla.

Tom ignored the jibe. "Except we can't go until that weird woman has left."

"What weird woman?"

"Your new best friend."

"Mrs Spark?"

"Yeah. She's cutting Mum's fringe. Plus, she brought some buns to apologize."

Orla groaned. Her head hurt. "Apologize for what?"

"For letting you go walkabout yesterday. She says she feels terribly guilty yadda yadda yadda. Anyway, Mum says you've got to show your face."

Orla sighed. She no longer owned her life. Then she

frowned. How did Mrs Spark know about yesterday? She glanced at Tom. "I'll be down in a moment."

Whatever fury Mum had been preparing to unleash on Mrs Spark for letting Orla go walkabout had vanished by the time she came downstairs. The pair were honking over tea and buns like a couple of old geese, mainly about how fabulous Mum's fringe looked. Dave was lying by the door. He lifted his head when he saw her, but only to give her a look of suspicion and disappointment.

"Have you recovered, dear?" asked Mrs Spark. "I feel terrible for letting you go like that yesterday."

"Lucinda, please," gushed Mum. "All's well that ends well and that's all that matters."

"Yes, but..." Mrs Spark was still trying to take the blame, but Mum wouldn't have it.

"Yes but nothing," she said firmly. "And I'm sure Orla would love to meet the society."

Orla glanced at the buns. They looked a bit heavy on the currants.

"What society?" she asked, opening the fridge.

"The Poldevel Historical Society," said Mrs Spark. "Monthly meeting today. I thought if I promised your mother that I wouldn't let you out of my sight for even a moment, then she might allow you to join us for a spot of tea. And a lot of fascinating talk about the parish records."

"OK," said Orla, somewhat nonplussed. She was supposed to be grounded but Mrs Spark had clearly changed Mum's mind along with her hairstyle.

The old lady stood up to leave. "Shall we say eleven thirtyish?"

"That'll be perfect," said Mum. She looked at Orla. "But you're not going dressed like that."

An hour later, Orla was standing on the doorstep of the old vicarage. There was a Land Rover parked next to Bessy and an ancient bicycle half buried in the wisteria.

The door creaked open.

"Perfect timing." Mrs Spark beamed. "Leave your stick on the step and follow me."

The hallway seemed even longer today and their footsteps on the parquet floor louder. The faded eyes in the black and white photographs watched as Orla trailed Mrs Spark, and she felt a sudden urge to turn and run. But it was too late.

"In here, my dear." Mrs Spark smiled, opening a door to reveal a gleaming mahogany dining table, around which old Mrs Perran and a much younger woman were sipping tea. They rose quietly to their feet as she entered.

"Ladies," said Mrs Spark. "May I present Miss Orla Perry?" She turned to Orla. "You've met Mrs Perran, but allow me to introduce Miss Teague. She runs the farm at Boskerry."

Miss Teague had wild blonde hair framing a face that looked like it had seen nothing but trouble. She was wearing a threadbare red dress that looked home-made and her pale blue eyes darted around the room like a trapped bird looking for an escape route. Her hand was trembling as Orla shook it, and there was a glint at her throat.

"Now then," said Mrs Spark, "I'm no longer going to pretend that this is a meeting of the local history society, although local history is very much our business. You don't drink tea, do you?"

"No, thank you."

"Water?"

Orla nodded, and as Mrs Spark poured water from a crystal jug into a dull green glass Orla swept her eyes around the table. They seemed more nervous than she was.

"What's this about?" she asked.

"I'm so glad you asked," said Mrs Spark, with the kind of smile people wear when they're about to tell you your grandmother has died. "Do you remember that sisterhood of like-minded folk I told you about the other day?"

Orla nodded.

"Well, my dear, this is it."

"Wow," she said. This was the army of witches: the

coven fighting the curse. They weren't quite as glamorous as she'd imagined. Or as numerous.

"It's just you three?" she said. "I thought there'd be more."

"There were," muttered Mrs Perran. "Apart from old Bron Meledor in Polgarrick we're pretty much the last survivors." She caught a sharp look from Mrs Spark and shrugged. "Oh, well. Can't be helped."

Mrs Spark took a deep breath. "You, Orla..." She reached across the table, gripped Orla's hand and looked her straight in the eye. "You are now part of that sisterhood."

Orla pulled her hand away. "Really?" she said. Surely there was more to joining a coven than going to a tea party? Didn't you have to dance around a bonfire under a Halloween moon or drink blood or something?

"I'm not sure I want to be."

"I don't think you have a choice," said Miss Teague in a quiet voice.

"Tell her," urged Mrs Perran. "Now is the time."

"Tell me what?" asked Orla. She could feel the world sinking to the pit of her stomach and her legs going weak like they always did when something bad was about to happen.

Mrs Spark looked at Miss Teague. "Perhaps you could begin?"

The nervous blonde woman frowned, coughed and then, avoiding Orla's gaze, started talking. Very slowly, as though reciting half-forgotten scripture.

"The story begins long, long ago, in the third millennium before Christ—"

"We haven't got time for all that," snapped Mrs Perran.

"Maybe fast-forward a tad," said Mrs Spark gently.

Miss Teague nodded. "Sorry. Let's start in the autumn of 1811." She looked at Orla. "You know the Carne Gang?" She spoke as though the infamous local pirates were still alive. Orla nodded. Miss Teague nodded back, then averted her eyes again.

"In the autumn of 1811, they attacked a Spanish treasure ship off Trinidad. She was the *Santa Cristina* and she was carrying around nine million pesos' worth of gold and silver." She sniffed. Quickly. Nervously. "Plus a passenger. A voodoo priestess called Caterina Jeudi. They were taking her from Cuba to Spain for execution…"

"But not before they'd tortured her into revealing the secrets of an extraordinary treasure," added Mrs Perran. She gave Orla a look so pointed it could have picked up leaves. "A rope of rubies. With a golden amulet."

"Yes." Miss Teague nodded. "Blyth stole it, but it killed him. Him and all his crew. His son, Cadan, was the only survivor. He sailed back into Carne in the summer of 1812,

111

quite mad. He gave that necklace to Pedervander Mazey."

"The fool had no idea what he had stolen," said Mrs Spark. "That necklace was older than Moses and one of the most powerful tools ever possessed by humanity. Whoever possessed it, and had the knowledge to unlock it, had immeasurable power – for good, or for evil."

"A magic necklace?" asked Orla. "Seriously?" She was trying her best to appear baffled. Not absolutely horrified that, until last night, the most powerful tool ever possessed by humanity had been under her mattress in a carrier bag.

Mrs Spark nodded. "Its proper name, according to the Zoroastrian texts, was Nagasalohita. It means 'blood serpent'. The rubies are from the Pamir Mountains in Central Asia and they have an extraordinary ability to soak up and store apparently infinite levels of energy. The Nagasalohita was sought by Cleopatra, by Alexander the Great, by Genghis Khan. The Venetians hunted for it. The Catholic Church spent billions searching for it. As did the Soviet Empire, the Nazis and the CIA. They've all been looking in the wrong places, though. They all knew it was a tool that could change the world, but the skill is in knowing how to release and focus that energy. Pedervander Mazey, it seems, had that ability."

"She studied the texts," added Mrs Perran.

"Of course she didn't," said Mrs Spark sharply. "I doubt

112

she could read English, let alone Zoroastrian. She was a born peller, and it came naturally. As long as she possessed the amulet, she could release the Nagasalohita's power."

"And she used its power to curse the land?"

"Correct."

Orla pushed back her chair. "Why are you telling me this?" she asked. "I'm on holiday. I'm just a tourist."

"No," whispered Miss Teague. "You're the special one."

"The *what*?"

"Tell her straight," snapped Mrs Perran, her blue lips as thin as a thorn scratch. She shifted forward in her chair to look hard into Orla's face. "You're descended from Pedervander Mazey, girl."

Orla shook her head. This was as mad as a chickenpox dream.

Mrs Spark held up her hand. "Hear us out, dear. It took five years to work out the bloodline and three years to find you. You're the one."

"But I'm from London," said Orla in a small, unconvincing voice.

"Yes, you are." Mrs Spark nodded. "Right back to the seventeenth century on your mother's side. But what do you know of your father's side?"

Orla flushed red. "My dad's in Africa," she said.

Mrs Spark nodded again. "I know," she said, gently.

"Your mum and he divorced four years ago. We know all this. But his great-great-great-grandfather was the son of Pedervander Mazey and a man called Cadan Leverick. He—"

"What?" Orla had gone cold. If this wildly improbable tale was true, then she'd seen her own ancestors last night.

"That baby boy was delivered to a widow in Zennor in August 1812. That's a fact."

"Why?" asked Orla.

"Because his mother had vanished," said Miss Teague. "There's only one testament to what happened, but it seems—"

"It seems," interrupted Mrs Spark, "that Pedervander Mazey disappeared without trace in the summer of 1812."

"What about Professor Gloyne's letter?" asked Miss Teague.

Mrs Spark held up her hand. "Don't drown the girl in irrelevant detail from an unreliable witness," she snapped.

Miss Teague bit her lip and looked at the floor. There was a definite tension between these two, thought Orla, as though they didn't trust each other.

"Who is Professor Gloyne?" she asked.

"She used to be one of us," said Mrs Spark, "but she's gone away."

"Like Pedervander?"

Mrs Spark looked at her. "Not quite. We know where Professor Gloyne is."

"You mean we hope we do," muttered Mrs Perran.

Mrs Spark gave an irritated little shake of her head. "The truth is that no one knows for sure where Pedervander Mazey went. Brittany is the most likely explanation."

"Or she turned into a crow and flew away," added Mrs Perran.

"None of that is what happened," whispered Miss Teague.

"What did you say?" asked Mrs Spark.

Miss Teague shook her head. "Nothing," she mumbled.

"Good." Mrs Spark smiled. "Shall we tell Orla about her kin?"

Miss Teague nodded. "The boy took the name Zephyr Boskethin and was passed off among the Zennor folk as an orphan from Penzance. He went to work in the Gurnard's Head mine when he was eleven."

"What about his dad?" asked Orla.

More looks went around the table, then Mrs Perran spoke. "Cadan Leverick drowned in 1812. His ship went down in a terrible storm off Gull Rock. August, it was."

"They say Pedervander conjured the storm that killed him," said Miss Teague.

"Because he betrayed her?"

"Because he came from rotten stock," muttered Mrs Perran.

"But he had a certain charm," said Miss Teague.

"I know," said Orla. "I've seen him." The words were out before she could stop them, and, but for a horrified gasp from Miss Teague, the local history society fell silent.

CHAPTER 15

Orla took a deep breath. The coven were glaring at her like a bench of hanging judges.

"I saw him last night," she said. "In a pub. I was dreaming, I think. He arrived late, and he was dripping wet."

Mrs Perran squeaked, and Mrs Spark held up a hand to silence her. Her chair creaked as she pulled it closer to Orla.

"Which pub, my dear?"

"It was called The Magpie," replied Orla.

"My God," breathed Mrs Perran. "She's talking about The Magpie in Tremarra. It closed when the boys didn't come home in 1919. Before that it was where the Carne Gang did their business. How could she know that?"

"Because I was there," said Orla. "Blyth Leverick and three others were there with Pedervander. She said Blyth paid her to protect them because Jesus wouldn't."

A gust of wind rattled the sash window and somewhere in the house a clock ticked. The three women stared at

Orla, who sat on her hands and stared back. She knew what she'd seen. Then Mrs Spark spoke.

"You've seen Pedervander Mazey?"

Orla nodded. "Three times. On the beach, on the cliff and in the pub. A crow took me."

"The Man in Black," whispered Mrs Perran.

"No," said Orla carefully. "A crow."

"That's Bucca Dhu," murmured Miss Teague. "We call him the Man in Black. He can appear as a crow – among other things." She looked at Mrs Spark with wide, terrified eyes. "She must really be the chosen one."

"Describe Pedervander Mazey," snapped Mrs Perran. She seemed angry. Or scared, like Miss Teague.

"She's tall, with long red hair down to here, kind of curly like mine. She has green eyes like mine and she was hurt. Badly." Orla drew her finger from her right nostril, across her mouth and down her chin. "She had a deep cut from here to here and she was bleeding from her side."

"What else did she say?"

"She said she'd made a terrible mistake and she didn't know if I was up to the task ahead of me."

"What task?"

"She said I'd have to work that out for myself."

Mrs Perran stared hard at Orla. "Was there a green flame?"

"Yep." Orla nodded. She didn't feel as confident as she sounded. She had a nasty feeling that the more she told these witches, the worse her day would get.

Gasps and glances whirled around the table like ghosts on a merry-go-round.

Mrs Perran glared at Mrs Spark. She'd seemed such a sweet old lady yesterday, thought Orla. Today, though, she was really quite scary. "Tell the girl," she ordered. "Tell her now."

"Ever since Pedervander Mazey cursed this land, folk have spoken of the green flame," said Mrs Spark. "They've seen it flickering out on the cliff and on Tregastenack beach. It's been seen here in Poldevel and at St Symphorian's in Veryan. The cunning folk always knew it was a manifestation of eldritch magic, but no one ever had the power to divine its meaning."

"What's eldritch magic?" interrupted Orla.

"Calls from beyond the grave," whispered Miss Teague. "A peller facing imminent death can send for help from the future."

Pedervander's magic lantern, recalled Orla, sending pictures through time.

"But the green flame has only been seen twice in the past twenty years," said Mrs Perran. "It seemed its power was weakening and thus it needed someone stronger and stronger to receive it. You must be an extraordinarily powerful girl." She pulled off her new glasses, closed her eyes and pinched the bridge of her nose like Orla's mum did when she was getting a headache.

Suddenly, her watery blue eyes snapped open and locked on to Orla. "Or an ordinary girl who has somehow found extraordinary power," she hissed. "Rather like Pedervander, don't you think?"

Orla threw the glare back at her, hard as flint, and the old lady flinched. The clock ticked. A chair squeaked. Miss Teague coughed, and then Mrs Spark placed both palms very carefully on the polished table. She looked at Orla, as though measuring her up, then at the coven.

"It's time she knew," she said.

"Knew what?" asked Orla.

"Why we brought you to Konnyck Vean," said Mrs Perran. "You have a job to do." The look on her face suggested that she had little faith in Orla's ability.

"You didn't bring me," argued Orla. "I came with my family."

"No, dear." Mrs Spark smiled. "We've been looking for Pedervander Mazey's descendants for years. When Professor Gloyne found you, we couldn't let you disappear, and who could resist a free week in a charming cottage by the sea?"

"Mrs Cottrall from church," gasped Orla. "Is she a witch too?"

"A peller, if you don't mind." Mrs Spark nodded. "I'm so sorry to have brought you here this way, but what choice did we have? Please tell me you're not angry with us."

Orla bit her lip. Of course she was angry, but at least the witches were being honest.

"What's the job?" she asked.

"Well, my dear," said Mrs Spark. "On the face of it, it's quite simple. The craft is a science. Everything we do requires huge amounts of energy – or sprowl. It flows around the earth like great underground rivers, and we know the places where it comes to the surface: at the meeting of waters, in blackthorn hedges and quartz rocks. The biggest part of our job is collecting the stuff. Then we have to coax it to do our bidding. That's what all the rituals are for. But with the necklace, you need neither sprowl nor spell. If you have a pure heart devoid of rapacious intention you simply need to be in the right place under a full moon, and in theory the necklace will absorb every last gram of that poisoned sprowl from the earth and allow the good sprowl to flow back in. The challenge is to find the right place."

"But why me?" asked Orla. "Aren't you the witches here?"

"Pellers," corrected Mrs Perran peevishly.

121

"Sorry," said Orla. "But you're the ones who know magic. Not me."

"And you're the only known descendant of Pedervander Mazey," said Mrs Spark.

"Apart from my dad and my brothers," argued Orla.

Mrs Perran shook her head. "Men are too weak for this work. It has to be you."

"Mrs Perran is right," said Mrs Spark. "If you can find the necklace we can use its power to reverse the curse. All the signs tell us it's hidden in this parish or the next, and it's obvious that Pedervander Mazey is trying to tell you, and you alone, where it is." She clasped her hands together, as though praying for Orla to agree.

"It's a big, big ask, Orla. I know." She looked at Miss Teague and Mrs Perran. "We all know. And we can't make you do it. Finding the necklace, and the hallowed place, must be your purest desire."

CHAPTER 16

Orla looked out of Mrs Spark's window, watching the low clouds rolling across the wet fields. *Give these witches their precious necklace and get on with your holiday,* pleaded a voice in her head. But another voice was more persuasive. *What if these ladies really are the custodians of evil, like Raven said? What if Mrs Perran—*

Miss Teague interrupted her thoughts. "You'll need a staff," she said. "For gathering sprowl."

"It appears that her staff has already found her," observed Mrs Perran. "Blackthorn, I believe."

"Oh," said Miss Teague. "But you'll need a familiar too."

"I'm sorry?" said Orla.

"A familiar is like a personal assistant," said Mrs Perran. "It can be anything with a face."

"It'll watch your back," said Miss Teague. "Guard your treasure."

Orla went cold as she realized she already had her familiar: a cheap rag doll from Spain with crazy hair who

123

was out in the wood keeping watch over the necklace.

"Anything but a dog," Miss Teague added.

"Ah yes," said Mrs Spark. "I'm sorry about what's going to happen to your dog."

Orla whirled around. "What?" she snapped.

Mrs Spark gave a sad little smile. "Remember how furious he got when I visited you at Konnyck Vean? Well, you're one of us now, and he's not going to like it one bit. Pellers and dogs are sworn enemies. When you hear all the dogs in a village start barking at two in the morning, you can be sure there's a peller out collecting grave dust for charms and blastings." She put a hand on Orla's arm. "I'm sorry, but your dog is going to hate you. It's a cruel price to pay, and I know you didn't ask for this. But it's your destiny, Orla. None of us could have prevented it. All we can do is try to protect you as best we can."

"Protect me?" Orla looked at each face in turn, searching for the twitch that would give away the guilt. "So who was protecting me yesterday?"

Mrs Spark looked puzzled. "I'm not with you, Orla."

Orla pointed out of the window. "In the wood over there. Something came after me."

"What?"

"I dunno. It was like this black shadow. Except it wasn't a shadow. More like oil or a liquid cloud. Or just pure nothingness. It came through the trees." She suddenly realized how utterly bonkers that sounded, but the alarm on the coven's faces proved they were taking her very seriously.

"There was someone there. A woman in black. She had a bucket of ashes. And a silver star around her neck." Orla pointed at Miss Teague. "Just like yours."

"This?" asked Miss Teague, fishing the necklace from inside her dress and holding it up.

"We all wear pentacles," explained Mrs Spark. "You should too, Orla. It's basic protection."

"How old was this woman?" barked Mrs Perran.

Orla shrugged. "Old."

"Build?"

"Tall. Thin."

Mrs Spark put a hand on her mouth. Miss Teague bit her lip. Mrs Perran closed her eyes.

"And you've seen this woman before?" asked Mrs Spark.

"I think she was lurking outside the cottage the night we arrived."

Eyes flicked back and forth. Miss Teague fidgeted. Mrs Spark made the face people make when they hear there's been a road accident.

"Menefrida Gloyne," she said.

"Must have broken out of hospital," muttered Mrs Perran.

"Excuse me?" asked Orla.

"A good peller gone bad," explained Miss Teague.

"Pure evil," muttered Mrs Perran.

"She's back because of Orla."

"Of course she is," said Mrs Spark. "But let's not panic."

"Er, panic about what?" asked Orla.

They all looked at her, like the village people must have looked at St George before he rode out to fight the dragon. Like the Israelites looked at David as he walked out to meet Goliath.

"Now then," said Mrs Spark, putting a hand on Orla's arm. "This isn't something we can't handle. We just need to be prepared."

Everyone else was looking at the floor.

"Does someone want to tell me who Menefrida whatever is?" asked Orla.

"Gloyne," mumbled Miss Teague. "Menefrida Gloyne."

"Professor Gloyne, you mean? You said you knew where she was."

"That was always a foolish assumption," sighed Mrs Perran.

"So who is she?" demanded Orla.

"Menefrida Gloyne is the peller of Polmassick," said Mrs Spark. "But she's dangerously deranged."

"Criminally insane is the proper term," said Mrs Perran.

"There was a time when we all thought Menefrida Gloyne had found the necklace," said Mrs Spark. "We were wrong, but she somehow had immense power. Orphaned at twelve, she was adopted by a widowed pig farmer from St Evan. Three years later, he was found drowned in the slurry pit. She lived on there for a couple of years. The bank sent two different men to repossess the farm. Both died."

"One was trampled to death by cows," said Miss Teague.

"Don't forget the meter reader," added Mrs Perran.

"And that couple from social services." Mrs Spark nodded. "That was especially gruesome, and Menefrida would have killed more if they hadn't taken her away."

"To prison?" asked Orla.

"Oxford University, actually," said Mrs Spark, raising an eyebrow. "She eventually became a professor of anthropology of religion. We truly thought she had found the righteous path, that we could work together. She's an exceptionally diligent historian – there isn't a parish record or ancient tome she hasn't read. It was her painstaking genealogical research that led us to you."

"Then people started dying again," said Miss Teague.

"In accidents," said Mrs Perran.

"They put her in the psychiatric hospital in Bodmin," added Miss Teague.

"Why didn't they put her in prison?" asked Orla.

Mrs Perran scoffed at the idea. "Since when has anyone ever proved anything against a peller in a court of law? They don't call us cunning for nothing, girl."

Mrs Spark shifted her chair to face Orla.

"Professor Gloyne is a dangerous woman who has dedicated her life to finding that necklace. Her quest has driven her quite mad, and that, combined with her dark talent, makes her a powerful force that we should all best avoid. What you saw in the wood sounds like Nulla."

A low rumble of assent went around the table.

"Nulla?" repeated Orla.

"The Night Mare," murmured Miss Teague. "It's almost impossible for one peller to conjure. You need grave dust from thirteen parishes and then—"

"I think we all know what it takes," interrupted Mrs Spark, "but I think that rather than going into technicalities we should all acknowledge that Menefrida has clearly discharged herself from Bodmin Hospital and returned here to make mischief. We cannot allow her to interfere in our work. Are we agreed?"

"Wait a minute," said Orla. She was beginning to lose track of this afternoon's absurdity.

The coven fell silent, waiting for her to speak.

"You think I'm the only one who can find the necklace because I'm descended from Pedervander Mazey, right?"

The three witches nodded.

"And if I find it, all I have to do is bring it to you and I can go home?"

More nods, only more vigorous this time.

"Fine," said Orla. "But before I agree, you need to show me what I'm up against. Prove to me how bad this so-called curse really is."

The three witches looked at each other, back and forth, before two pairs of old eyes came to rest on Miss Teague.

"What do you expect me to do?" she cried.

"Give Orla the tour," said Mrs Spark. "And do be gentle with her, would you?"

CHAPTER 17

Miss Teague drove her Land Rover at high speed along narrow lanes hemmed in by high banks and overhanging with dripping leaves, braking every now and then to allow steamed-up tourist cars to squeeze by.

After several miles of what felt to Orla like a roller coaster ride, the Land Rover lurched onto a muddy track. "You want to see what the curse has done?" asked Miss Teague. "Boskerry Farm is the place to start."

It looked exactly like any other Cornish farm: a big farmhouse surrounded by stone outbuildings. Miss Teague parked outside the house and climbed out of the Land Rover, her red dress flapping over her green wellies. Orla followed, glancing despairingly at her school shoes.

"Oh. Yes. I see." Miss Teague nodded. She opened the back door of the car and pulled out a pair of green rubber boots. "Better put these on. They might be a bit big but you'll manage."

Orla pulled them on, picked up her staff, then shuffled

across the farmyard to where Miss Teague was standing beside a stone wall. She looked like a frightened rabbit waiting for a barn owl.

"See those fields?" she said. "We used to have two hundred cows in them, but we couldn't keep the curse out." She bent down, tore a handful of wet grass from the ground and held it out to Orla. "Looks good, doesn't it? But there's no goodness in it. The cows could eat this all day but the quality of the milk just kept falling."

She slipped through the gate, followed the wall for a few steps and then bent to lift something from the grass.

"This is a thunderstone. A fossilized sea urchin. In other places, one or two of these is enough to protect an entire farm from evil. Here, we have hundreds of them." She bent again, and picked up another. "There's probably a thunderstone every five yards in every field in this farm, but they weren't enough. Never enough."

She tugged a loose stone from the wall, reached into the gap and pulled out a rusty chain that was threaded through a tube of white bone – like the one Orla had seen at Mrs Spark's house.

"Is that part of a dog's backbone?" she asked.

Miss Teague seemed impressed. "It is," she said. "You catch a nice dog, or dig up a dead one, charm its bones and spread them around. It's powerful protection, but not

131

here." She leaned over the wall. "See this?"

Making a mental note never to bring Dave to Miss Teague's farm, Orla looked over the wall. All she saw was weeds.

"That's travelling pearlwort," announced Miss Teague. "It's a plant that always protects cows. Everywhere except here."

She strode off. Orla followed.

"I used to come out here every spring with my grandmother," she said. "We'd dedicate new charms and recharge the old ones. They never worked."

She crossed a stone stile into the neighbouring field. The grass, Orla noticed, was different here. It was yellower, coarser, and choked by knotweed, nettles and thistles. It sloped downwards, thinning into bare, black mud where, at the lowest point, there stood a grey steel-fenced enclosure topped with barbed wire. As they approached, Orla shivered. She could feel the malevolence.

"Behind that fence there's a natural sinkhole," revealed Miss Teague. "They used to call it Lagasowmor. It means 'eyes of the sea'. It's fed by an underground river that flows from St Ketherick's Wood up on the moor. The water came crystal clear from here once, but sometime in the nineteenth century it stopped flowing. They say the seaward side collapsed, preventing water getting out or in. Now it's a deathtrap."

She took a few reluctant steps towards the fence. A big yellow sign said *Danger to life. Drowning hazard. Do not enter.*

"My brother was one of those that died here," said Miss Teague. "Lemuel was his name. He was ten years old. I was fourteen. No one could understand why he came down here in the middle of the night, during a thunderstorm, to drown in there." She kicked a loose stone and it clanged off the steel. "No one except my grandmother. She knew why. Evil sucked him in."

She nodded towards the steel. "You can't see from here, but that hole drops straight down for a hundred metres, and there's another thirty metres of poisonous sludge at the bottom. The council tried to fill the hole in. They poured thousands of tonnes of concrete in and it made no difference, so the best they could do was build this fence." She gave Orla a wet-eyed smile. "How could we have been stupid enough to think stones, bones and cowslips could protect us from power like this?"

She began walking back up the slope.

"When did Lemuel die?" asked Orla, struggling to keep up in her oversized wellies.

"Ten years ago this month. I can tell you in days if you want."

* * *

They drove on, past Trehays and St Erin. At Polmassick, Miss Teague pointed at a tall yew hedge on the edge of the village.

"Menefrida Gloyne's place," she said. "She was just twelve years old when she came home from school one day and found her mother dead at the parlour table. Victim of a poppet blasting. You know what that is?"

"Nope."

"You make a rag doll," said Miss Teague. "We call it a poppet. Then you take a part of someone: some hair, some clothing or some fingernail, and you attach it to your poppet. Then you use the poppet to pass pain or death on to that person. Only a peller could have killed old Mrs Gloyne."

"Maybe Menefrida did it," suggested Orla.

"Impossible," said Miss Teague. "I mean, literally impossible. A peller can't bewitch her own mother. It had to be someone outside the family."

"I thought you pellers were a sisterhood," said Orla.

Miss Teague threw a nervous glance around the vehicle, as though she might be overheard. Her voice dropped to a whisper. "You heard what Mrs Spark said: that necklace is one of the most powerful tools ever possessed by humanity. There's more than one peller around here who would kill for it."

"Like who?" asked Orla.

Miss Teague shook her head. "Conversation over."

She gunned the Land Rover and hummed a manic tune as she sped along the twisting lanes. Orla watched through one eye, expecting a car full of tourists to come round a blind bend at any moment. Miss Teague clearly didn't trust Mrs Spark or Mrs Perran any more than she trusted Professor Gloyne. But then again, she was also completely crazy.

Orla pulled a ball of newspaper from her pocket. "Can I show you something? I meant to at the old vicarage but I forgot." She unwrapped the package and held the contents in the palm of her hand.

Miss Teague glanced over, and saw the green stone in Orla's palm. She slammed the brakes on.

"Where did you get that?" she gasped.

"Pedervander left it for me. She said it was proof that our meeting was more than a dream. My brother found it and I bought it from him."

The car behind was honking its horn but Miss Teague was oblivious. She looked worried. "You should have told us about this," she said.

"I'm telling you now, aren't I?"

Miss Teague crunched the Land Rover into gear and drove on. "You should have shown it to Mrs Spark and Mrs Perran."

"Why?"

"Because it's a memory stone. It holds memories." She shook her head in disbelief. "Pedervander Mazey's memories, for goodness' sake. She must have known the fire would fade – that she wouldn't be able to appear to you any more – so she backed it all up in quartz."

"How do you get the memories out?" asked Orla.

"With a ritual. You need hallowed ground and the hare to open it up, but you need to do it at the exact top of the full moon. It's extremely difficult. It needs wreathing in smoke from a burning holly branch first to purify it, and you'll need more sprowl than you can imagine." She threw Orla a sidelong glance. "Forget it. Even I couldn't be sure of getting it right and I've been learning the craft since I was half your age."

"Shall we take it to Mrs Spark?"

"Yes." Miss Teague nodded. "But not yet. She told me to show you around first."

"Isn't this more important?"

Miss Teague seemed confused. Scared, even. "Yes. No. I mean yes, but she told me to show you around."

Driving one-handed, she scratched her head as though suddenly attacked by fleas. "Must be gentle," she muttered. "What to do?" She mumbled for another mile or so, before driving off the road and onto a village green. She killed the engine then turned to Orla with what she probably hoped was a reassuring smile.

"Welcome to Polgarrick."

It was a pretty village even in the rain, thought Orla, its huddle of slate-roofed cottages peeking out from behind gardens of swaying hollyhocks. A brook ran through the green and the Cornish flag was flying from the tower of the tiny church. Miss Teague wound down her window and pointed out of the Land Rover.

"See that robin?" she asked. "He was kidnapped. We have to catch birds from miles away and release them here so the tourists think we have some, but they never last long."

"What happens to them?"

Miss Teague sighed. "They can feel the wickedness in the air so they fly away fast or they die. Come on. I'll show you around."

They walked down the high street. It was eerily quiet but for a tiny, white-haired old lady dragging a shopping trolley.

"That's Bron Meledor," said Miss Teague, giving a wave that wasn't returned. "She's the village peller. Half blind, deaf as a post and the only true Cornishwoman left here. Once there was a peller in every village, but they're like the birds. They fly away, or they die. See that sign?"

She pointed to a plaque on the wall of the nearest cottage. It read *Property of Cornish Country Holidays*.

"Or this one…"

"Sea and Country Cottage Rentals," read Orla.

"Or Cornish Breaks, Cornwall4U, West Coast Retreats, and so on," said Miss Teague. "Every single house in this village, except for Bron's place, the pub and the shop, is a holiday home, because all the real Cornish people have moved away."

"Why?"

Miss Teague sighed. "Because of the curse, silly."

She scooped a stone from the parapet of a garden wall and showed it to Orla.

"This is a hag stone. It provides all-round basic protection against evil intent. Tourists take them away as souvenirs, so Bron's job is to replace the missing stones and keep them charmed. The problem is that she's ninety-seven this year and her health is failing. She fell sick a few weeks ago and got behind with her duties. This is what happened." She stopped beside a cottage swathed in green tarpaulin. As it flapped in the wind, Orla could see the black smoke trails around the broken windows and the charred timbers beneath the broken roof.

"There was a family of six inside," said Miss Teague. "Tourists from Oxford. Luckily, they all got out. The fire brigade said it was an electrical fault." She hugged herself and walked on, but Orla grabbed her elbow.

"Wait," she said. "Why couldn't it have been just what the fire brigade said it was? An electrical fault. A simple, random piece of bad luck? Why does everything that happens here have to be connected to the curse?"

"Because it is," hissed Miss Teague. "If you'd spent your entire life here, watching houses burn and crops fail and trees fall and children die, you'd know." She poked Orla in the chest. "You're just like any other tourist. You see nothing. Have you looked around Konnyck Vean? Have you seen the precautions we've had to take to keep you and your family alive in that evil house?"

"No," said Orla.

"Look around. There are sparkle jars under the sink. Adder bones in the curtain linings. Hag stones behind the books. Charm pouches under the mattresses."

"I think Tom found one of those," admitted Orla. "We thought it was potpourri."

"Tell you what," snapped Miss Teague, "why don't we take all the charms hidden around this cottage here and see what happens? It'll probably be all right for a few hours, perhaps even a whole day. Then a kid will get run over. Or a mother will fall down the stairs. Or the kitchen will go up in flames. Bron will think it was her fault, that she forgot to swap the stones over, so we'll be OK. What do you think?" She put her hands on her hips, her eyes bulging and red circles burning her cheeks.

Orla stared back, then shook her head. "No," she said. "But you need to show me more proof."

"Fine," said Miss Teague. She ran her tongue across her teeth as if trying to reach a decision, all the time looking at Orla. "I'll take you to St Ketherick's Wood up on the moor," she said at last.

"Where's that?"

"Very close to hell."

CHAPTER 18

Standing at the altar in a stone circle high on the cloud-shrouded moor, her hair hanging like rats' tails, her hands red with cold and a crazy witch standing behind her begging protection from death, Orla was wondering why she hadn't gone to the monkey sanctuary with Mum and Tom.

They'd parked the Land Rover far below, climbing on foot through swirling clouds and squelching bog to find this rain-washed circle of quartz.

The ritual was essential if they, as pellers, were to survive St Ketherick's Wood, said Miss Teague. The preparation had involved fire and stone and knife and bone, an offering of Cornish gin and a lot of running in what Orla now understood to be the sinistral direction. Now she was standing in an ancient compass circle with her back to a gap in the rocks that Miss Teague called the Serpent Gate. Orla felt an entirely inappropriate desire to laugh, and it was made worse because Miss Teague was taking it all so seriously.

Without touching Orla, she encircled her with a bunch of hazel branches she'd cut from the hedge far below, swapping them from hand to hand as she whisked them around and around from head to toe and back again, all the while chanting, *"Hekas, hekas, este bebeloi! O theoi genoisthe apotropoi kakon!"*

"Now you do me," she whispered. "You're exorcizing evil. We need to be sure we're pure before we seek protection. Just pass the hazel around me in the sinistral nine times. Be sure not to touch me and never look through the Serpent Gate."

It was easier said than done, but Orla played her part.

"Now the fire," whispered Miss Teague. A muted crack, like a tree snapping in half or a boulder dropped from a great height, came through the murk, followed in rapid sequence by two more. "We must be quick," urged Miss Teague. "The wood knows we're here." She drew her knife and knelt beside the lantern, holding the blade against the flame.

"We summon thee, Sarf Ruth. Breathe into our blood and spark our cunning. We conjure thee."

From somewhere out in the mist came a moan so low that it was more felt than heard. It made Orla's stomach tremble. Her knees were shaking and her legs felt so weak she could have simply toppled over. She wanted to look behind her, but that would have meant peering through the Serpent Gate.

Miss Teague raised her arms, closed her eyes and, in a low, trembling voice, said, "We conjure thee, red spirits of the east road. You are the guardians of the flame of sight and the blade of cunning and the forces of protection. Hear our call, awake from your rest and come to us."

At last, her eyes snapped open.

"Ready?" she asked. She looked more nervous than ever. That wasn't a good sign.

Orla nodded, even though she didn't feel particularly ready. The protection ceremony in the compass had left her feeling giddy, with dry mouth and clammy hands. Her legs felt heavy and her fingers numb. And she had no idea what to expect in the wood.

She grabbed her staff and jogged to catch up with Miss Teague as she strode downhill through the tussock grass.

"What's going to happen?" she asked.

"The wood is cursed," replied Miss Teague. "It's also sentient. It will sense that we are pellers and that we mean it harm, so it will try to defend itself."

"How?"

Miss Teague stopped, half turned, and took Orla's wrists in her cold hands. "It will play with our minds. Make us angry. Crazy. Scared. Then it will try to kill us."

Orla felt suddenly sick. "So, er, why are we going?"

143

"Because you asked for proof, silly. But if you're scared, that's fine. I can have you back in Poldevel within the hour. Just say the word."

The clever part of Orla's brain liked the sound of that. Go back to Poldevel and have a Cornetto.

"Nope," said her stupid mouth. "Let's do this."

A three-metre wall of wet granite, topped with jagged shards of broken glass, marked the wood's perimeter. Miss Teague led Orla around it until they came across a pile of rocks lying in a breach. It looked like the evidence of an attack on a castle.

"We'll walk in until you feel it. As soon as you're convinced, we'll turn around and walk out." She held out her hand. "Take it, and don't let go while I'm still breathing. That's important."

Hansel and Gretel, thought Orla. Hand in hand through the enchanted wood.

They climbed the pile of rubble and descended on the other side.

"Mind the sheep," warned Miss Teague.

Half a dozen soggy clumps of wool and bones lay across the path. "Most of them stay well away," said Miss Teague. "But sometimes an especially stupid one gets curious, and the wood sucks it in. The blood vessels burst in their brains."

Stupid sheep, thought Orla, suddenly gripped by a weird, burning anger. Stupid Miss Teague with her stupid hair. Stupid, soaking, freezing Cornwall. Stupid, stupid world.

Gripping Miss Teague's hand, she noticed that the trees looked like those she'd seen in books about World War I – shattered limbs and shredded trunks reaching for a sun that never shone. As they stepped over a poisonous-looking stream, she stretched out to take a piece of peeling bark, but Miss Teague dragged her away.

"Are you stupid?" she snapped. "Don't touch anything."

"I was just checking," retorted Orla.

"Well, don't," hissed Miss Teague.

They walked on, hand in hand. Orla felt her ears pop, and she was finding it harder and harder to draw enough oxygen into her lungs. The drizzle seemed like acid scorching her skin and the earth beneath her feet crackled like broken glass.

"You're hurting my hand," she told Miss Teague.

"Stop whining," snarled the peller. "It's your fault we're in this place."

"Really?" asked Orla, with as much sarcasm as she could muster – and she was very good at sarcasm. "This was your idea, actually. I didn't ask to come here and go through all that stupid mumbling and praying."

Miss Teague stopped, jerking Orla's arm. "Stupid mumbling and praying, is it? Without it, the wood would have killed you before you'd gone ten paces. Together, we might be just strong enough. Apart, we're finished. Now grip harder, weakling."

Orla tried, but her strength was draining like bathwater spiralling down a plughole. Above her, the bare branches seemed to lean inwards in an evil embrace, the twigs and boughs interlacing like overlaid spiders' webs. Her boot caught on a root, and she stumbled, dropping her staff.

"Get up," hissed Miss Teague.

Orla shook her head, seeing the trees blur. She saw someone digging. Then the image was gone.

"I can't," she gasped. "I need to rest." She was shivering, not with cold or with fever, but as though she'd been bitten by a snake. She gasped lungfuls of air and watched as something black flitted across the edge of her vision – too big to be a crow. Another followed, the draught of its passing icy against her neck. She snapped her head from left to right, the panic bubbling up like the froth in a shaken Fanta bottle. The trees seemed to be roaring like a gallows mob, but somewhere behind their screams she could hear voices shouting her name. It was Tom, and Richard and Mum. They must have come up here to rescue her. And there was Dave – a black and white flash scurrying through

146

the holes in the fog, his nose to the ground, searching for her. She tried to pull her hand free, but Miss Teague was stronger.

"I have to go," Orla cried, her feet scrabbling in the black earth.

The dark things screeched past, catching her hair, and as she tried to brush them away she saw the rock in Miss Teague's hand.

"Stay still, little witch. Stay still while…"

She pulled Orla towards her, but Orla pulled back, gaining enough ground to grasp her staff. She felt the power, the stored-up sprowl, flooding her veins, and with a snap of her wrist she yanked Miss Teague to her knees. But the rock, with a point like a pick, was still raised.

"I need to tap thee, girl," whispered the peller, "to release thy spirit."

As the rock came down, the sprowl felt like ice water in Orla's throat. She stared Miss Teague straight in the eye. "Drop it," she growled.

Miss Teague's arm froze. Her eyes widened as though she'd seen the Devil himself and the stone fell to the ground. Still gripping the other's bony hand, Orla dug the staff into the soil and dragged herself to her feet. She saw Dave again. He was just over there, lying on his side, wet with rain, eyes glazed and deathly still. She needed to save him, but to do so she would have to let go of Miss Teague's hand, and that would mean certain death. The trees were swirling faster and faster around her, and as she took a step she fell, into a crack in the earth. Miss Teague's hand was slipping away, her strength gone. Orla gripped harder, pulling against the peller to get back to her feet. She looked for Dave, but now the forest floor was thick with yellow smoke.

"Get up," she told Miss Teague. "We have to find my dog."

"It's OK, Orla." She smiled, her expression that of a well-meaning aunt. "It's just a dream, silly. All you need to do is let go and you can wake up. Then –" she leaned close to Orla, her blonde hair hanging like wet ropes across her face, her hand closing around Orla's wrist –"then you will find your dog. He's not here. He's waiting for you to wake up. Just let go of my hand."

Of course it was a dream. What else? Orla smiled as the relief surged through her body. Let go, wake up, pat Dave, go downstairs and make toast. She smiled at Miss Teague, and their eyes met.

"It's not a dream," cried Orla, snatching Miss Teague's free hand from her wrist and strengthening her own grip. The wood was taking over their minds, turning them against each other, trying to kill them, and if they didn't get out right now, Orla realized, it would probably succeed.

Holding her staff in front of her like a lance, she started walking, dragging Miss Teague behind her. She knew it was exactly two hundred and sixty-eight paces to the breach in the wall because she'd counted them. It was a skill she'd learned reading a book about the SAS, and Orla counted down as she dragged Miss Teague behind her.

But there was a big problem. It went like this: "Two hundred and thirty-three, two hundred and thirty-two, two hundred and thirty-one, two hundred and thirty, two hundred and twenty-nine, two hundred and sixty-eight, two hundred and sixty-seven." It was like walking the wrong way down a travelator – every exhausting step towards safety taking her further into the evil wood.

It was only when she closed her eyes that she saw the stream: no longer poisonous, but cool and silver. It seemed perfectly normal that it was flowing uphill, and Orla followed it, past the dead sheep, and onto the moor. The air was suddenly full of oxygen and as the shrieking in her head diminished, she dropped Miss Teague's hand and fell, exhausted, to her knees. Then she raised her head.

Up there on the ridge, near the compass circle, the scudding clouds parted for a moment. Just long enough for Orla to see the woman in black.

CHAPTER 19

The Land Rover was where they'd parked it, but Orla walked straight past, eyes unblinking. A picture was flickering like a broken TV: black soil, brown leaves, white plastic, and she couldn't shake it.

She kept going until she emerged from the clouds, and then, propping herself against a wet boulder, she took ten deep breaths. She was awake. She was alive. And she was now convinced that something very, very wicked was happening here.

The rumble of a diesel engine came out of the gloom, and then the Land Rover appeared on the track. It stopped and Miss Teague, her eyes as red as if she'd been crying for a month, emerged. She paused at a safe distance, as though scared to come closer. She touched her hair, wiped her lips with the back of her hand and stared sideways into space, searching for words.

"You saved my life, Orla Perry," she said at last. "And I tried to take yours. St Ketherick took my soul and,

God, I tried to..." Her mouth opened and closed, like a goldfish. She wobbled, then sat down heavily on the wet grass, shaking her head as the tears rolled down her face.

Orla stared back. She never cried, but she managed to give Miss Teague a tiny smile.

"No one died," she said. It was a phrase her dad had often used to describe their chaotic days out together, but it made the weeping even worse, and Orla wasn't sure how to react.

The image flickered again.

There was a hole in the ground. Not here, on the moor, but far away, in the leaf litter of another wood. A wood where Ozymandias lay. The wood where she'd hidden her rag doll to keep watch. Was Malasana calling?

Orla turned to Miss Teague. "Get me home, please," she said. "Right now."

Miss Teague could hardly drive for sobbing, so it was a relief when Orla spotted Bessy speeding in the opposite direction, lights flashing in urgency.

Mrs Spark was in no mood for pleasantries. She looked Orla up and down then snapped, "Wait in Bessy and clean yourself up. There are wet wipes in the glovebox."

Then she shouted long and loud at Miss Teague before slamming the Land Rover's door and marching back to the car, getting in and telling Orla to put on her seat belt.

"Obviously you'll keep what you saw today to yourself," she ordered.

She looked terrible, thought Orla, her face drawn, her lips bloodless and her eyes red and sunken. But then again, Orla probably didn't look much better.

"Ordinary folk don't need to know."

"I'm not used to keeping secrets from my mum," said Orla. That wasn't strictly true. But escaping from a cursed wood with a deranged witch who had tried to kill her was in a different league from having a secret stash of Jaffa Cakes in her jumper drawer.

"I'm sure you'll manage," said Mrs Spark.

"She was up there," said Orla. "Professor Gloyne. I saw her."

Mrs Spark stared at Orla, long and hard. "Are you absolutely sure about that?"

"Absolutely."

"It could have been a hiker."

"It was Professor Gloyne," insisted Orla. "She must have followed us."

Mrs Spark shook her head. "How could she have known?"

"I don't know, but the stream was running uphill. She must have made that happen. It's how I got out."

Mrs Spark shook her head. "Menefrida Gloyne would not have wanted you to get out of that wood, and Miss Teague was too weak. *You* made the stream run backwards, Orla."

"No, I didn't."

Mrs Spark slowed down as they approached a bend in the road. "Yes, you did. You may not know it but deep down, far behind the tiny bit you use to think with, your brain has realized that the things ordinary people believe to be unchangeable – gravity, day and night, even death – can be manipulated." She looked at Orla. "You have no idea how powerful you are, do you? You've not only lived to tell the tale of St Ketherick's Wood, but you have survived the worst that the most powerful peller in Cornwall could throw at you today. She won't be pleased, so we cannot lower our guard. She will conjure more powerful blastings now. There will be deaths."

Orla bit her lip. "What are blastings?"

"Black magic. Summoning Wisht Hounds, releasing spirions and the like. The kind of stuff a whole coven would struggle to achieve even if it had the justification. Menefrida Gloyne can call it up just like that." She snapped her fingers. "Can you imagine what she could accomplish if she had the Nagasalohita?"

"Can't you teach me a spell I can use against her?"

"Absolutely not. The craft isn't something to be dabbled with. Things can go terribly wrong." She glanced at Orla. "Have you heard of the Rule of Threes?"

"Nope."

"Whatever you send out will return to you threefold. So if a peller wishes, say, a toothache on someone, that peller will get it three times worse. It keeps a lid on the use of blastings, but Menefrida Gloyne is apparently immune." She gripped the steering wheel a little tighter and sighed. "Honestly, Orla, I don't know if we can beat this. I don't know if the Nagasalohita is really still here, or if the curse can ever be lifted or if there's even any point in carrying on this fight." She sounded for a minute like she might cry, but instead she sniffed and threw Orla a little smile. "Think I need a holiday," she said. "Serifos in Greece would be nice. It's a magical place."

Water was dripping from the trees as they bumped down the track. Mrs Spark checked her watch.

"Five minutes early. Not bad considering." She pulled a hairbrush from Bessy's glovebox. "You look like you've been dragged through a hedge, child. At least let me try and make you presentable for your mother."

Orla winced as the old lady dragged the stiff bristles through her curls, yelping as they caught on the knots.

"Bit better," muttered Mrs Spark. She cast a critical

eye over Orla's second destroyed dress of the week. "I'll distract your mother while you go and change. Try and hide that rag in the car and I'll wash it and repair it as best I can." Then she sprang from the car and strode cheerfully towards the cottage, waving and hollering hellooos like a maniac.

A true professional, thought Orla, wishing she could just crawl into bed with a bar of Dairy Milk. But first she had to check if Malasana really had been calling. Because if she had, it could only mean one terrible thing.

CHAPTER 20

The necklace was gone. Biting back the panic, Orla looked up at Malasana, high in an oak where she'd been tied to keep watch.

"Who took it, Mala?"

The rag doll seemed to be staring deeper into the wood.

Feeling the sweat on her spine, Orla followed her gaze. She saw the carrier bag lying ripped on the leaf litter, and then she saw Richard. He was leaning against the fallen oak looking as smug as a student teacher on his first bust. Raven was sat on a protruding branch, all shiny in PVC jeans and a sparkly black mohair jumper.

"Well, well, well," said Richard. "If it isn't the notorious jewel thief come to check her stash."

Orla's mouth opened but nothing came out.

"I knew you were up to no good. I heard you going out while you thought the rest of us were sleeping. Couldn't help but follow you."

"What have you done with it?" hissed Orla.

Raven jumped out of the tree. "You've been busy," she said.

Orla glared at Richard. "Where's my necklace?"

"We had a little rummage through that so-called holiday cottage today," said Richard. "It was like searching a Russian hotel room for bugs. That red thing Tom found? It's magic, apparently. There are hundreds in there. Jars full of dead birds under the floorboards. Chains of razor blades behind the curtains. Bones. Fossils. Stinky liquids. Weird, weird stuff."

"Not weird. Just standard protection charms," said Raven. "It's witchcraft, Orla. Like I told you."

Orla took a deep breath. "You have no idea what you're messing with."

"I think we do," said Raven.

"No." Orla shook her head. "You really, really don't." She glared at Richard. "Where's the necklace?"

"This, you mean?" He dangled the red stones in front of her, the golden amulet shimmering in the middle. "I think you'd better start talking, Orla." He ran his fingers over the stones.

"You shouldn't be touching it," warned Orla.

"Says the thief," said Richard.

"Seriously," she said, her voice rising. "It could really hurt you."

"Maybe you should listen to her," said Raven. "She actually looks pretty scared."

"Yeah?" scoffed Richard. "Really? Like it's going to suddenly turn into the death serpent from hell and strangle me?"

He raised the necklace and dropped it over his head, lurching towards Orla like a zombie and letting out a mocking gurgle, as though the life was being choked from him. Then he stopped walking, and his eyes went very, very wide. His mouth opened and closed.

"Take it off, Ri—"

Orla didn't finish her sentence, because as she was speaking Richard flew backwards as though struck by an invisible wrecking ball. He hit Ozymandias with a sickening thud, and slumped to the ground.

Orla dashed to her brother's side. His eyes were half open, and there was yellow drool dripping from his chin. She snatched the rubies from around his neck and threw them into the leaves. Richard's tongue lay fat and swollen against his teeth, and his eyelids flickered as he struggled to speak.

"What the hell are you up to, Orla Perry?" he croaked. Then he passed out.

An icy calm came over Orla. She felt for a pulse. Nothing. She tipped Richard's head back, peering into his mouth for obstruction. Then she looked at Raven.

"Can you do CPR?"

Raven nodded. "You blow; I'll pump."

Kneeling in the leaves, Raven placed the heel of her right hand on Richard's breastbone, clasped it with her left, and rocked her entire body weight against it. She performed six quick chest compressions, then nodded at Orla, who pinched Richard's nose and blew two lungfuls of air into him. There was no response, so they repeated the procedure twice, three, four times more. By now, Richard's lips had gone blue, his skin cold. They were too far from Konnyck Vean to call for help. If they couldn't restart his heart within the next couple of minutes, it would be too late to save him.

A freshening wind rustled through the treetops and somewhere near by a crow let out six measured squawks. Orla resorted to punching Richard's chest in frustration, then blowing air into him so fast that she felt faint. At least two minutes had passed, and he was growing colder, deader, by the second. It was no good.

No good at all.

They couldn't save him.

But maybe the blood serpent could. Orla darted over to where the Nagasalohita lay in the leaf litter, placed it around her neck and grabbed her staff. Raven gazed in astonishment as Orla stood over her dead brother and raised her staff above her head.

"With the necklace, you need neither sprowl nor spell,"

Mrs Spark had said. Could it really be that simple?

"Fix him," she hissed at the snake of rubies. "Fix him right now or I'll take you to the top of the cliff and toss you into the sea." To make perfectly clear to whom she referred, she whacked Richard in the chest with her stick.

But it made no difference.

He stayed dead.

The crow fluttered overhead.

Then Richard coughed.

Twice more, and suddenly his eyes grew wide, as though he'd taken a ride to hell and back on Menefrida Gloyne's Night Mare. Then he saw Orla, and the necklace around her neck.

"Get it off!" he screamed. "It will kill you!" He scrabbled at the ground, trying to stand. "We need to get back to the cottage. We need to tell Mum what's happened. It knocked me clean out."

"It killed you, actually," said Raven quietly. "Your heart stopped. Your sister saved your life." She covered her mouth with her hand. "I can't believe I just saw that."

Orla looked down at the necklace in her hands. "It's called the Nagasalohita," she said. "I found it in this tree. It was put there more than two hundred years ago by a witch called Pedervander Mazey. She cursed this land with magic so powerful that it became self-replicating, expanding through the soil and contaminating the land, the people and the wildlife. It kills bees and makes crops fail and sheep's brains explode. It makes dogs fight each other, drives people insane and it kills the phone signal, and the only people who can stop it are us, because we're the direct descendants of Pedervander Mazey, and that's the reason we ended up here on holiday instead of going camping in France like I wanted to."

Richard stared at her for a long, long time. "You're totally bonkers," he said at last.

"I believe her," admitted Raven. "I saw what that necklace did to you and I saw how she used it to revive you. And I know that there's something very evil here."

Richard shook his head. He stepped across the stream, as though trying to put space between two worlds.

"If there's any truth whatsoever in any of this, then we're not the people to fix it. Trust me. The government has people..."

"The government has people?" scoffed Raven. "You think there's some secret agency tasked with eradicating black magic? Hasn't been one of those since the eighteenth century."

"There's no such thing as magic," seethed Richard. He was wobbling a bit, as though he could collapse again at any moment.

"I wish that were true," said Orla. She stepped into the flow, stabbing her staff into the stream bed.

"What are you going to do?" asked Richard, rubbing his chest. "Turn me into a believer? I don't think…" The words fizzled out, but his mouth stayed open and his eyes grew very large.

"How the hell…" His gaze snapped from the stream to Orla. "How the hell are you doing that?"

Orla looked down. The stream was rushing back uphill, its flow reversed. As if by magic. "Oh, that," she said. "Sorry, got distracted. You were saying?" She pulled her staff from the stream bed and the water flowed back downstream.

"Jesus," whispered Raven.

Richard shook his head. "No. It's impossible. It's contrary to the laws of physics." He grabbed his hair with both hands. "Maybe it's me. Maybe I'm ill."

Orla shook her head. "You were dead not so long ago, but you're absolutely fine now." She stabbed her staff back into the stream bed, partly to check that she could reverse the flow again and partly to see if she could make Richard's and Raven's eyes bulge any wider. She succeeded on both counts, and she gave a modest little smile.

"You should see what I can do on a broomstick," she said. "Tomorrow I'll explain everything I know, but

162

between now and then, I really, really need to sleep. I've had a very busy day. Can you two keep your mouths shut until then?"

Raven looked like a girl who'd slammed the front door and seen her house collapse. Richard looked like he'd been upstairs in the bath when it happened. They nodded, slowly at first, then vigorously. They were onside.

CHAPTER 21

Mum didn't get up the next morning. Migraine, she said, so after making her some green tea, Orla led her brothers and a very suspicious dog to the fallen oak, where Raven was waiting. Orla sat them down and told them the whole story, from the discovery of the necklace, to her meetings with Pedervander Mazey and the Poldevel coven. No questions were allowed until she had spoken of the Night Mare, the horrors of St Ketherick's Wood, and the dark menace that was Menefrida Gloyne. Then she told them about the curse – how it had spread beneath the surface of the county, like venom creeping outwards from a snakebite – and why she, Orla Perry, great-great-great-great-great-granddaughter of the woman who had caused the problem, had been called to solve it. To kill the curse, allow the ghosts to rest and let the life return to the land.

"And that's it," she finished, scanning their slack-jawed faces for a reaction. "Any questions?"

Dave was giving Orla the look he gave postmen. Tom's mouth was opening and closing.

"Can you do spells?" he finally asked.

Orla shook her head. "Not really. I can do some stuff but I don't know how it happens."

"Can you tell what the winning lottery numbers will be?"

"No."

"Is that stone you bought off me something to do with this?"

Orla nodded. "It's a memory stone. It belonged to Pedervander."

"Memory stone?" asked Richard.

"It's like a witch's USB stick. Stores memories."

Tom nodded at Orla's blackthorn staff. "Is that stick your wand?"

"Sort of," said Orla. "It's called a staff. But it's not like you think."

"Oh my God," he exclaimed. "This is so like a film."

"It's not," snapped Orla. "This is real life."

"What are we going to do with the necklace?" asked Richard.

"I haven't a clue. I was thinking I should give it to the pellers but now I'm not so sure. Pedervander said I have to be sure I'm doing exactly the right thing."

"We can't hide it in the cottage," argued Richard. "It's too dangerous."

"True," said Orla, feeling a flush of guilt. The Naga-salohita killed the unblessed like slow poison, Pedervander had said. No wonder everyone had been so sick on this trip. "But I've got an idea where I can stash it."

"Where?" asked Raven.

Orla shook her head. "I'm not telling you that. If you don't know, no one will be able to torture it out of you."

"Torture?" gasped Tom.

Richard shrugged. "What if something happens to you?"

Orla shrugged. "If I die, then there's nothing you can do but go back to London."

"Die?" yelped Tom. "We're supposed to be on holiday."

"I've got a question," said Raven.

"Uh-huh," sighed Orla. Her head was beginning to ache.

"How are you going to defeat the curse?"

Orla cut a circle in the leaves with the point of her staff. "I have absolutely no idea."

Raven nodded. "That's what I thought. C'mon. We need a plan."

Tregastenack beach was empty but for a well-wrapped couple walking a Border collie. The clouds raced fast and low overhead, threatening another downpour.

"We need to get online," said Richard. "Do some deep research into this Pedervander person."

"Forget about it," said Raven. "There'll be no 4G until the curse is lifted."

They were close to the couple now, and the collie had spotted Orla. It went berserk, throwing itself between Orla and its owners, barking and snarling like the last line of defence between an orphaned lamb and a pack of slavering wolves.

Dave shook his head sadly. The collie seemed like a clever and loyal chap, and he'd clearly sensed the same weirdness radiating from Orla that Dave had been trying to ignore. The collie's instinct, quite reasonably, would be to attack her, but if he tried that he'd be going home in a veterinary ambulance.

"I'm so sorry," gasped the man, struggling to attach the lead to his dog. "He's never ever done this before."

His wife smiled helplessly, but Orla noticed the suspicion in her eyes.

The kids hurried past, and the dog's feverish barking was drowned by the roar of the wind and the crash of the surf. The first raindrops began to fall, and Tom knew where to take shelter. He jogged ahead to the fist of granite bisecting the beach.

"In here," he called, beckoning the others towards a

cleft in the rock. "Someone keeps their boat in here but I've never seen them."

"There's a boat in there?" asked Raven.

Tom nodded. "Like a rowing boat. Smugglers, probably. And there's something else even cooler."

"No, there isn't," said Richard, peering inside with some distaste.

"No, really," protested Tom.

"No, really not," said Richard. "It's dark and it stinks of dead fish."

"Let's go to my place," suggested Raven.

Dark curtains of rain were falling across the sea as the five reached the big rock where Orla had first met Raven.

"Hey, look," cried Tom. "You can go inside."

"It's the Lightning Shelter," said Orla. "It was built in 1818."

"Cool," he said. He bobbed down, went inside and came straight out looking like a rabbit after a near miss with a python.

"There's a tramp living in there," he gasped.

Raven sighed. "*I'm* living in there. Come in. Can't offer you tea and cakes, though."

The shelter was cold and dark, but at least it was dry.

"Why the heck are you living in here?" asked Richard. "I thought you were staying at a caravan park."

"There is no caravan park," said Raven, fiddling with a candle lantern. She glanced at Richard shyly. "I lied to you. Sorry."

"So you've been in here the whole time?"

"One night only."

"What happened to your tent?" asked Orla.

"What tent?" asked Richard.

"Gone." Raven shrugged. "Something really weird ripped it to bits so I moved in here." There was a scratch and hiss as a match flared. Raven touched flame to wick, and yellow light danced across the four faces.

"What happened?" asked Orla.

Raven met her gaze. "Black dogs," she said in a low, quiet voice. "Silent black dogs that came through the gorse like a tidal wave. They tore everything to shreds. I ran." She pointed at a black backpack. "My escape bag is all I took."

"Jesus," muttered Richard. "If the farmer set the dogs on you just for camping on his land we should report him."

"They weren't that kind of dog," said Raven.

"Wisht Hounds." Orla nodded. "Sent by Menefrida Gloyne."

"Which hounds?" asked Richard.

"No," said Orla. "Wisht Hounds. They're a blasting."

"A curse," added Raven.

"Then we should report her," said Richard. "That's attempted murder."

"I think if Menefrida Gloyne had been attempting murder then Raven would be dead," said Orla. "The Hounds were sent to scare her away."

Tom glanced around the low, wet cave. "How long are you going to stay in this hole?"

"Just until I find out what this place did to my dad," replied Raven.

An awkward silence followed. Raven stared through the low door to where the rain was bouncing off the muddy footpath. "Why won't your dog come inside out of the wet?" she asked.

"He's on guard," said Orla. She didn't add that Dave couldn't stand to be near her any more. "I need to get out of the house tonight. I need to find Pedervander Mazey."

"We're coming with you," said Raven. She looked at the boys. "Right?"

"No," said Orla. "It's too dangerous."

"Life is dangerous," said Raven.

"That is such a goth thing to say," noted Tom.

"We're coming with you whether you like it or not," said Richard. "The only question is: where exactly are we going?"

Orla gave them a fierce look. The three glared back more fiercely. She was outnumbered.

She took a deep breath. "Fine. We're going to look for the green flame."

"The green flame?" echoed Raven. "You mean the green flame that's only been seen twice in twenty years?"

"Maybe it will appear more often now that Pedervander knows I'm here," said Orla, knowing as she did so that she was talking rubbish. The flame was sputtering. Pedervander was fading, and she'd told Orla herself that there would be no more dreams.

"We need more research," mused Richard. "If we can't get online, then you need to ask your witchy friends at the local history society for more background."

"Professor Gloyne is the only real historian in the society and she's trying to kill us," said Orla. She put her head in her hands and groaned. "This is ridiculous. We haven't got time for all this. Pedervander talks in riddles. She keeps saying the deed must be conceived and performed by one pure of heart and devoid of rapacious intention. Mrs Spark talks of the full moon and a hallowed place, but that's all I know. We need more clues. We need to contact Pedervander again and find out what happened before she disappears for ever."

"How, exactly?" asked Raven. "We don't even know where she's buried."

"Use the stone," said Tom. "It's got her memories inside."

The Lightning Shelter fell silent. Candle flame flickered.

Outside, Dave ate an earwig. Inside, Tom gave the others a sidelong glance, frowning at their incredulous expressions.

"What?" he cried.

Orla gave him a bear hug. "Tom Perry, you're a genius."

A low woof came from outside.

"Dave's spotted hostiles," said Richard.

Raven peered out from the cave. "Civilians," she whispered. "We should go."

They crawled out of the Lightning Shelter and trekked in single file along the cliff path, nodding polite hellos to the party of hikers as they passed.

Once they were alone again, Richard grabbed Orla's arm. "Show me this stone," he ordered.

Orla pulled the small bundle from her backpack. Unwrapping it, she held it aloft, gripping it like a walnut between her thumb and forefinger.

"Is that it?" he muttered. "It's a bit small."

"How does it work?" asked Raven.

"There's a ritual."

"A ritual?" repeated Richard, one eyebrow raised.

Orla nodded. "Miss Teague told me. Something about summoning the hare at the top of the full moon on hallowed ground."

"There's a lot of hallowed ground and full moons involved in this witchcraft game," observed Tom.

"And what exactly is the top of the full moon?" asked Richard.

"The lunar zenith," said Raven. "It's when the moon is at its highest in the night sky. And it's tonight, by the way."

"Seriously?" asked Orla.

Raven nodded. "If we don't do it tonight, we'll have to wait a month."

"Do we have to dig up a corpse?" asked Tom.

Orla ignored him. "At St Ketherick's it involved a fire, a knife, some alcohol…"

Richard dropped his head and let out a long sigh. "Jesus," he said. "This is devil worship. We're going to hell."

Raven shook her head. "It is not devil worship. It's witchcraft. There's a big difference."

"I can see the headlines now," he groaned. " 'Tourists were devil worshippers, say Cornwall police.' 'Infamous Four were satanists'," he added. Then he caught Dave's glare. "Sorry, Infamous Five."

"But aren't we trying to do a good thing?" asked Tom.

No one replied. They were too busy trying to absorb the absolute gravity of an utterly absurd situation – like being mugged by clowns.

"What we're doing is good, isn't it?" repeated Tom. "Orla?"

Orla reached for his hand and squeezed it. "I think it's good," she said.

"It'd better be," said Richard. "But for the record I want it to be known that I have serious concerns about this whole enterprise."

"We'll sneak out tonight when Mum is sleeping," said Orla.

"What if she wakes up and finds we're not there?" asked Tom.

"Tell her you're going for a sleepover at my place," suggested Raven.

"I think she'll want to see your fictional caravan first," said Orla.

"If your mum wakes up and you three are missing, she'll call the police," Raven pointed out.

"She can't," said Richard. "No signal, remember?"

"Even so," said Orla. "We need to make sure she sleeps very deeply, and I know exactly how to make that happen."

"Are you going to put a spell on her?" asked Tom.

"That won't work. A peller can't bewitch her own mother, but there are herbs that will do the job."

Richard let out a gasp of exasperation. "Jesus. Welcome to Orla World, the place where you drug your own mother."

"There's one more snag," said Orla. "I don't know how to perform this ritual. But Mrs Spark will."

CHAPTER 22

Richard took Mum a cup of green tea in bed and announced that her loving children were going to prepare a three-course dinner to say thank you for arranging such a wonderful holiday. Mum looked worried, but was too weak to argue. Plus she couldn't resist the opportunity to meet the mysterious Raven. The menu was to comprise Richard's roast chicken, Tom's ice cream (which wasn't Tom's at all but Ben & Jerry's) and Orla's knockout salad.

As the four prepared for their shopping expedition, Dave watched their every move. Everything Orla did these days filled him with fear, and that was a feeling he really wasn't used to. A big part of him wanted to bark at her until he was hoarse and then hide under the bed, but he was a professional. The kids, on the other hand, were complete amateurs embarking on a venture with a high risk of hostile contact. Worse, if they split their force, he wouldn't be able to protect them all. Richard, who was usually quite sensible, wanted them to stay together. Orla wanted to work alone.

"I need to speak with Mrs Spark," she said. "And I need to gather sprowl. I don't know how much I'm going to need tonight and I can't take you three with me. We'll meet back here later."

"I'm coming with you," announced Raven.

"No, you're not. You're getting the bus to the super-market with the others."

Idiots, thought Dave. He made a quick risk assessment. Orla was the most vulnerable, because she was operating alone. He'd have to swallow his distaste and go with her.

"And Dave goes with you too," said Orla to Tom. "He likes public transport and I can't take him with me."

Nice, thought Dave. Tied up outside Tesco while all hell broke loose.

Orla left Raven with the boys and a very grumpy dog, and set off to Poldevel to see Mrs Spark. She would know exactly how much hops and valerian Orla would need to put Mum into a lovely deep sleep, and precisely how to open the memory stone.

But first she had to hide the Nagasalohita.

She vaulted the wall into the churchyard and started scanning the headstones. Fourth row from the back, third from the left, she found what she was looking for.

CAPT. MARTIN HEMMING
Master of the *Adventurer*
Drowned off Tater Du
8 August 1820
At Rest

Clearly not a victim of the curse, though, thought Orla, otherwise he'd have been in the Old Ground. Accidents, it seemed, still happened. She rummaged in the weeds until her hand closed around the cold iron shaft of the church key.

The ancient wooden door creaked open, and the sprowl hit Orla like a blast. It hissed from the floor like a detuned TV, the signal distorted by distant yet urgent voices. Sweat broke out on her forehead, her fingertips were going numb and she wondered if stashing the Nagasalohita in a sacred place was such a good idea. But that was what Pedervander Mazey had told her, so she gripped her staff, took a deep breath, and paced up the nave between the empty pews, looking for a hiding place.

The further she moved from the door, the more painful the white noise became. By the time she reached the transept, the pain was so intense that she thought her teeth would fall out, and then she understood. Taking the Nagasalohita to a Christian altar was like trying to push the like poles of two magnets together. The blood serpent clearly wanted to sleep close to the fire, but not this close.

A noise like a sigh made her turn, her staff held out like a sword, but the church was empty. Then she saw the font, and got the message. The Nagasalohita wanted to lie beneath, protected by enchanted water, and just as she somehow knew the rubies would give her the strength to move the font aside, she knew there would be a vault beneath.

The font slid away as though on greased wheels, revealing a stone-lined chamber. Orla carefully placed the necklace into the void, replaced the font, then scanned the church for a suitable lookout spot for Mala. She'd be happier here than she had been in the woods. Gypsies loved churches.

Three minutes later, Orla was at the old vicarage. The rain swept over her like a wire broom, streaming off her yellow sou'wester and soaking through her jeans. Her hair hung in rats' tails around her face, and her hands were red with cold.

She marched across the gravel and knocked on the door. Then she noticed that Bessy wasn't there.

"Drat," she muttered, knocking again anyway. Longer, harder. No reply. She glanced at the rear garden wall. Mrs Spark would understand, she thought, scaling the ivy-covered bricks like a cat burglar and dropping silently into the garden on the other side. Two minutes later, she was back with a pack full of hops and valerian, but without a clue what to do next. Mrs Spark could be gone all day.

Then a light bulb lit up in her head.

She'd go and visit crazy Miss Teague at Boskerry. She didn't know whether the peller would be in a fit state to receive visitors after the St Ketherick's Wood terror, or if she would even be home, but what other choice did she have? It was five miles, more or less, across country to Boskerry and that, she realized with a sigh, meant a ten-mile round trip.

In the pouring rain.

It was in the wood outside Poldevel when she realized she was being followed, but after what had happened the last time, she didn't call out. Instead, she kept walking until she reached a huge, flat field with nowhere to hide. Then she stopped abruptly and turned.

Her stalker was caught in the wide open.

"Oops," said Raven sheepishly.

"Go away," growled Orla.

"Where are you going?"

"None of your business."

"I'm coming with you."

"No, you're not."

"You can't stop me," insisted Raven, rather unconvincingly. She was talking to the girl who could bring the dead back to life and make water run uphill.

Orla tightened her grip on her staff.

Raven took a step closer. "What were you doing in the church?"

Orla was shocked. "Were you spying on me?"

"Don't tell me you hid the necklace in there?"

"Go away."

"No," said Raven. "You need me to watch your back."

Orla shook her head. "I can manage fine on my own, thanks."

"That's what they all say," sighed Raven.

"All who say?"

"All the dead people."

"Look, I haven't got time for this," snapped Orla. "Go home, Raven." She turned and walked away, dragging her staff along the hedge to harvest its sprowl.

"Are you really that stupid?" yelled Raven. "Whatever drove my dad crazy out in that ocean is obviously the same thing you're trying to stop on dry land. Let me help you. Please. And maybe you can help me."

The desperation in her voice made Orla pause. She turned, stabbing her staff into the grass.

"I know you want to find out what happened to your

dad, but you have absolutely no idea how dangerous this place is."

"Yes, I do. I saw what attacked my camp."

"That was nothing," said Orla. "If you come with me, there's a very good chance you'll die and no one – no detectives, no coroners, no doctors – will ever be able to prove it was anything but an accident."

Raven's eyes flicked to the left, then back to Orla. "That's a risk I'm prepared to take," she said. "And whether you like it or not, you need my help. Please."

Orla stared at her. "What's your real name?"

Raven stared back. "What's that got to do with anything?"

"It's a matter of trust."

"No one gets to know my real name," growled Raven.

Orla shrugged. "Fine. Bye-bye."

Raven scowled at her. "It's Joan," she muttered. "Joan Baqri."

"Joan Baqri?"

"Yes," hissed Raven. "Happy now?"

"I prefer Raven," said Orla. "Let's go."

"Where are we going?"

"To visit a witch."

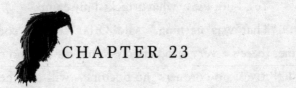

CHAPTER 23

By the time the pair reached Boskerry they were as wet as drowned sailors.

Her heart fluttering, Orla approached the green front door. She paused and looked around, half expecting a Wisht Hound to spring from nowhere, and then, before she could knock, the door opened.

Miss Teague looked terrible. Her hair was wilder than Orla's and big black rings encircled eyes still puffy from weeping. She kept one hand on the jamb and the other on the door, pushing her face through the crack between.

"Why have you come?" she whispered.

"To see you," said Orla.

"To kill me?"

"Er, no, actually. I need your help."

Miss Teague stared at her for a long time. Then her red eyes rolled towards the other girl. "Who's that?"

"It's Raven."

Miss Teague studied her, long and hard. "She's a menkolon, isn't she?"

"I have no idea what you're talking about," said Orla impatiently. "We need your help."

Miss Teague shook her head, one eye on Raven. "I see a trap. Have you and your raven come to kill me?"

Orla sighed. "I think we've covered this already. The answer was no, remember?" Now she'd stopped walking she was beginning to shiver. And her head ached so much she felt sick. The curse was wearing her down.

"But you know, don't you?" hissed Miss Teague. "I know you know. And you know I know you know."

"Know what?" Orla could feel a vein beginning to throb in her temple.

"Aha." The witch smiled. "Know what, indeed?"

"Look," began Orla, taking a step towards the door. It slammed shut. "Brilliant," she sighed. "What's a menkolon?"

"Never mind," said Raven. "Knock again."

Orla knocked again. An upstairs window opened and Miss Teague stuck her head out, her hair swinging in the wind.

"What do you want?" she called.

"We need some advice," Orla said slowly. "We want to open that memory stone."

There was a long pause. "A memory stone, you say?"

Orla nodded. "Yep. The one I showed you yesterday. The one you said needed a complicated ritual. Remember?"

Another long, cold, wet pause, then the window clunked shut. There was a thumping on the stairs, and the door opened. Just a crack.

"Leave the staff outside," ordered Miss Teague. "What's in the bag?"

"Just the usual stuff," said Orla. "Notebook, pencil, penknife, first aid kit, torch, a camera, plastic gloves, some hops and valerian and a bit of rope."

"Show me."

Orla slipped off her backpack, opened it and let the peller rummage through. Miss Teague thrust it back at Orla, then waved the pair into the farmhouse. Orla went first, her nostrils twitching with odours so strong she could taste them. As her eyes became accustomed to the dark, she saw the bones: hundreds of them, stacked on the stairs, arranged on a high shelf and dangling from hooks on knotted ropes. Sheep skulls, rabbit spines, fox shins and cow ribs, all bleached white, some painted with strange characters.

"Love what you've done with the place," said Raven.

"Go through to the parlour," said Miss Teague. She pointed to a doorway hung with a curtain of vertebrae which jangled as Orla pushed through. The smell was even stronger in here: camphor, mugwort, benzoin, patchouli and fear.

Lots of fear.

Orla glanced around the room, checking for exits, noting the charms and the bones piled on the table, the dresser, the mantelpiece and the windowsill. Charm bags like the one Tom had found at Konnyck Vean hung like Christmas decorations; in the spaces between the bones there were stones; and the rough wooden table in the centre was crammed with bottles and jars of oily liquids, berries and razor blades. And, noticed Orla, a box of Crunchy Nut Cornflakes and a faded postcard saying "Greetings from Slough". And just in case the notion that this was the home of a paranoid sorceress hadn't yet crossed the visitor's mind – and Orla doubted there were many of those – a huge, black cauldron hung from an iron tripod over the hearth, steam rising from its lip.

"Take a seat," mumbled Miss Teague, gathering a bundle of seaweed from the single bed that ran along one wall. "Bladderwrack," she said, by way of explanation.

As Raven perched on the edge of the bed, she knocked a spool of red wool to the floor. It rolled away like a stream of blood. Miss Teague gasped, bent to gather it up then changed her mind.

"Not safe," she whispered. "Not safe at all." She bustled back and forth, picking up sticks, rearranging bunches of herbs and dried flowers and trying to slide various knives out of reach without being noticed. The entire situation was a bit awkward, thought Orla, as Miss Teague made a feeble attempt to tidy the glassware on the table.

"Sparkle jars," said the peller. "They're powerful protection. Usually." She held up a green bottle. "Would you like some gin?"

"I'm fine, thanks," said Orla.

"What about your raven?"

"Raven's fine too."

Miss Teague nodded, then turned her attention to the cauldron. A gust of wind thumped the window, and a chain of rat bones rattled.

"You've got loads of lovely charms," said Orla.

"Not enough," muttered Miss Teague. "When she comes, she'll cut through them like a chainsaw."

"When who comes?"

Miss Teague laughed, short and sharp. "When who comes, indeed," she scoffed, but as she did so, she glanced nervously out of the window and reached, almost unconsciously, to touch a long wooden box on the mantel-piece. "You think I'd invite her by saying her name in my own home?" Her eyes snapped to the wooden box. She snatched it up and turned to Orla. "Know what this is?"

Orla shook her head.

"It's a coffin." She was crazier than ever, thought Orla sadly. Maybe she'd made a mistake coming here.

"A tiny coffin for a powerful spirit." She grabbed the bottle of gin with her free hand and took a slug. Then, opening the coffin lid, she let a few drops dribble from her mouth onto what lay within.

"Mandragora," she whispered, lowering the coffin so Orla and Raven could see. Inside, a grotesque vegetable doll with a crudely carved face stared blankly back. "Mandrake root, you'd call him. House spirit is what I call him. Or Trevor. Sometimes I call him Trevor. He's two hundred and thirty-six years old. Came from the foot of Five Ways gibbet. Every new moon, I take him out, bathe him in gin, then wrap him in silk. In return, he keeps the evil at bay." She shut the lid gently and replaced the coffin on the mantelpiece.

"See this?" Miss Teague was now holding up a tiny, grimy glass bottle. "Aspercum powder."

"Oh," said Orla.

"Got a cat?"

"Nope."

Miss Teague shook her head. "You should have a cat. Shares the burden." She looked around the parlour wistfully. "I had one until recently. He ran off. Oh well." She slammed the bottle down on the table. "Take it."

"What for?"

"For your cat."

"I told you," said Orla. "I don't have a cat."

"Ah, yes." Miss Teague nodded. "But you will, and one day, when you find it lying dead in the road, you'll thank me for aspercum powder." She made a stirring motion with her finger. "You lay the cat at the west gate of the compass – Death's gate. Purify, summon the toad…" She rummaged in an earthenware pot and handed something black and crispy to Orla. "That's a toad. Keep it safe. Then mix the powder with a drop of blood, pour it into the cat and it will be revived. They say you can do it eight times, but I've never seen it work more than twice. Cat's never dead till it's buried."

She picked up the bottle and pushed it into Raven's face. "Tell her to take it."

"Take it, Orla," said Raven, raising her eyebrows in a "let's get the hell out of here" way.

"Thanks." Orla grimaced as she slipped the desiccated toad and the bottle into her backpack.

"Better take this too," muttered Miss Teague, putting another bottle into Orla's hand. "Oil of the moon. If your cow gets lost, the oil will find it. Got to be bleeding, though."

"I haven't got a ... oh, never mind," she sighed. It wasn't worth the effort to reason with the woman. She took the bottle. "Thanks."

There was a long silence. The smell grew worse. The bones rattled. Orla smiled politely, but Miss Teague wasn't watching.

"Do you sleep in this room?" Orla asked finally, just to make conversation.

Miss Teague spun around to face her. "Why do you ask?"

"It's a big house, that's all."

"Just me. My grandmother died two weeks after Lemuel. We left a year later. Daddy couldn't take the loss, what with the stress of keeping the farm going and all. Moved to Slough. He died five years ago. Broken heart, they said. Mum doesn't go out much any more. Just to the shops and back." She picked up the postcard and stared at it as though it held a clue as to what she should do next. "I came back and I wish I hadn't."

"Who's Lemuel?" asked Raven.

Miss Teague gazed at the space between them. "My little brother," she said at last. "Lagasowmor took him, ten years and seven days ago. I could tell you in hours, if you want."

Raven glanced at Orla. "Who's Lagasowmor?" she asked.

189

"That steel cage thing in the valley," said Orla. "That's Lagasowmor. It's—"

Suddenly, Miss Teague dashed across the parlour like a terrier smelling a rat.

"Show me your hands," she snapped at Raven.

"What?"

"Show me your hands," hissed Miss Teague. "It's you, isn't it?" She twisted her head to look at Orla. "It was said she would come, and here she is, with you. Suddenly it all makes sense."

"Does it?" said Orla.

The witch stabbed a trembling finger at Raven. "She'll have lines of intention, you mark my words. Show me. Now."

Raven clasped her hands behind her back. "I will not," she said.

Miss Teague stared hard at her, eyes like drill bits, her breath coming in short gasps. Raven stared back. Miss Teague licked her lips, then nodded.

"I see now. That's good. And bad. You lied to me. Now we know where we stand." She flung the parlour door open. It screeched as it scraped across the floor.

"You can go now." She was staring at the flagstones. "Please leave now."

"Not yet," said Orla. "You need to tell me how to open that memory stone. We—"

"No," said Miss Teague. "Deal's off. You tricked me and I caught you out. Just go now!"

Orla glanced at Raven. Raven rolled her eyes.

"I actually don't know what you're talking about," said Orla. "We didn't come to trick you. We just need the spell."

Miss Teague shook her head. "No, no, no. You need to go."

Hugging herself, she stepped away from the open door, shuffling around the table to be closer to her hearth. And her most powerful charms. She gave Orla a sad smile, like a death row prisoner who'd accepted her fate.

"She will kill us all – you and your raven included, girl. There were others before you. All the charms in Cornwall couldn't keep them safe. They all died. You'll be next, after me. You and her. You need to go now. Right this minute."

Orla walked around the table and stood close enough that Miss Teague would feel her words as much as hear them.

"No," said Orla, in a menacing, Dave-like growl. "You don't get rid of me that easily. I've just walked two hours in the rain to find you, and I'm not going back empty-handed because you're randomly freaked out." She reached around Miss Teague and grabbed the coffin from the mantelpiece. She really didn't want to do it but asking nicely wasn't working. She pulled the mandragora root from the coffin and dangled it over the cauldron. "Either you tell me, or Trevor gets cooked," she threatened.

"You wouldn't," gasped Miss Teague.

"She would," said Raven. "She's crazy."

"Don't," cried Miss Teague. "I'll give you everything you need for the ritual. But you must promise one thing."

"Fine." Orla nodded, handing over the root.

"You never come here again. Ever."

Orla held out her hand. "Deal," she agreed.

CHAPTER 24

The kitchen at Konnyck Vean looked like a First World War operating theatre. Knives, bowls and spillage covered every surface and the floor was scattered with peelings and screwed-up kitchen roll. Richard, clad in a stained apron, looked like the harassed surgeon, his face red and his hair awry.

"Where've you been?" he asked as Orla and Raven slipped in. Dave gave them both a filthy look, then stuck his nose under his tail.

"Gathering information and fetching these," Orla replied, making a gap on the table for a bag of wild leaves and a squid-like valerian root.

"Dave did a wee on the bus," said Tom. "Then he went mental outside Tesco when some old lady tried to stroke him. It was so embarrassing."

"Poor you," said Orla distractedly. "Where's Mum?"

"Soaking upstairs in artisan bath oil we got on special offer," said Richard. He glanced at Raven. "Nice day out?"

"Bizarre, actually," she replied. "Major case of mistaken identity with a deranged witch. She seemed to think I was an assassin."

"You'd make a good assassin," observed Tom.

"Thanks," said Raven. She picked up the valerian root. "Do we need all of this?"

Orla shrugged. "Better safe than sorry. I'll make the salad."

She dug out the colander, tipped in the leaves she'd picked on the way back from Miss Teague's house, washed them and carefully arranged them in four individual bowls. Sorrel, wild garlic, dandelion leaves, chickweed, watercress and the liquorice-flavoured leaves of ox-eye daisies. In a fifth she combined all of the above, plus a big handful of bitter hops and grated valerian from Mrs Spark's garden. Hopefully, it would send Mum into a deep and restful sleep with lovely dreams. Thinking about it that way made Orla feel better, but only slightly.

Dinner was no triumph. Orla forgot to make a dressing for the salad, so they had to use ketchup. Richard's roast chicken had the texture of an old football and his potatoes looked like lumps of coal. Tom's ice cream was fine, because it wasn't his but Ben & Jerry's, but Mum was too busy interrogating Raven to notice the shortfalls.

Orla watched Raven as she answered Mum's questions. She was good, but when she thought no one was watching, her face betrayed a profound and immovable sadness. Raven had lost her dad, and no matter what happened here, he would never be coming home.

"I cooked, so Orla washes and Tom dries," announced Richard as the meal ended.

"I can wash up," offered Raven. She was looking for an escape route, thought Orla.

"Not at all," said Mum. "You're our guest. Orla and Tom will do it."

Tom gave Orla a smug look. "You know what that means?"

"You can't do that," protested Orla. "Not now."

Tom shrugged. "Sorry. Not my fault. The deal was twenty jobs, and by my reckoning you've got seventeen to go." He poked Orla and mouthed "And I don't care if you are a witch."

Orla glared back. There had to be a spell for this.

As Orla washed and dried, the others watched the news. Mum was struggling to stay awake and didn't notice the report from St Michael Penkivel Church, where health and safety officials were urgently examining the medieval stonework after a local woman, seventy-eight-year-old

Adelie Perran, had been killed by a falling gargoyle as she tended a grave. Orla went hot, then cold. She felt sick. She bit her lip and concentrated on scrubbing the roasting tray. Tending a grave indeed. Mrs Perran was gathering grave dust more like, but why in a parish so far from Poldevel?

Then she got it. Grave dust from thirteen parishes was needed to raise the Night Mare.

Had Mrs Perran been working with Menefrida Gloyne?

Mum stood up and stretched. "It's been a fabulous evening, kids, and it was a real pleasure to meet you, Raven. I love your look. Used to be a bit of a goth myself once." She tried and failed to stifle a cavernous yawn. "You guys can stay up, but I'm absolutely exhausted and my head is still thumping." She gave Tom a goodnight kiss and waved at Orla. "Richard, you will walk Raven back home, won't you?" She yawned again, then frowned. "Where did you say you were staying, Raven?"

"The caravan site at Trevorna," lied Raven.

Mum nodded. "Lovely. Don't forget to lock up, you lot."

The conspirators made eye contact as Mum climbed the stairs, but none spoke a word. They waited forty long minutes, then crept upstairs to make pillow dummies for their beds. Five minutes later, Orla, Tom and Raven were waiting by the back door. Dave glared at them from his basket, furious to have been told he wasn't needed on the mission.

"We've got forty-one minutes before the zenith," said Raven. "We need to go."

"Where's Richard?" hissed Orla.

"Doing his hair and trying to decide which shoes to wear," whispered Tom. "He can't choose between the brogues and the pixie boots."

Fortunately for Richard's pixie boots it wasn't raining, although the low sky looked as if it could give way any minute. Invisible behind the clouds, August's full moon was reaching its zenith as the quartet walked like soldiers across the wet grass to Poldevel Church.

Skirting the churchyard, they walked down the lane to the Old Ground, where generations of pellers had been buried beneath the black slate gravestones with their runic carvings.

Richard shuddered. "I like the graves in the churchyard better."

"These are more powerful," said Orla.

The sprowl here was like an earth tremor: constant, rumbling, teeth-jarring. On flat ground between the slates, she laid out the tools she'd taken from Miss Teague: knife and stone; fire and bone; copal; frankincense, juniper and lavender oil; oak bark; sage, rosemary and verbena; dried yew berries; Epsom salts and a pewter vial containing a tincture called fire of the moon. She also had her staff, a compass-plotting cord, a tine from a stag's horn, a moon thread for power, the dried skin of a hare and, from the pocket of her jeans, the memory stone and the neatly folded page of handwritten instructions. And a corked bottle of gin.

She glanced at Richard, who shook his head in weary disbelief, then at the church clock. It was five minutes to midnight.

"Thirteen minutes to go," said Raven.

Orla nodded. "Let's get started."

CHAPTER 25

A mile to the west, Dave was in a fix. He'd been looking for an escape route since the kids had locked him in. Following his nose upstairs to find an open window, he now found himself balanced rather precariously on the bathroom windowsill. A bottle of cut-price artisan bath oil lay cracked and bleeding on the floor, but that was the least of his worries. Getting out of the cottage involved jumping from an upstairs window, and Dave, being a dog of low elevation, disliked heights. The more he stared down into the blackness, the more he realized that this was a stupid idea.

But instinct told him that the people it was his duty to protect were getting themselves into serious trouble. Yes, he had deep concerns that Orla had gone over to the dark side, but a security professional never let personal opinion get in the way of duty. Dave looked down, trying to form a plan.

After three long minutes, he realized there was no plan. So he jumped, plunging head first into a plastic rain butt with such force that he tipped it onto its side. As the foul green water drained away, Dave stepped out of the butt and shook himself, a bit like James Bond shooting his shirt cuffs. Now he was going to find those stupid kids.

Those stupid kids were sitting in the Old Ground. The clouds had gone, and, for the first time this holiday, the stars were out. But they were too disappointed to notice. The ritual simply hadn't worked. Orla had followed the instructions to the letter, using incantations and smoke inside her carefully prepared compass circle to summon the hare, but it hadn't shown and the memory stone had lain there as useless as a broken light bulb.

Orla was furious. Mrs Spark was right: the craft wasn't something you could dabble with. You couldn't just read a spell from a book; and now, with her ham-fisted fumbling, she had messed up the only chance she had of contacting Pedervander Mazey.

"Dammit," she cried, slapping her wet legs. She'd blown it. And now the dogs were barking all over Poldevel. It seemed they could smell failed witches too.

"Can't we try again?" asked Tom.

"No," said Orla. "Moon's past the zenith." She started packing up the useless tools of her ineffective conjuring. "I messed up."

"At least you've still got the necklace," said Richard. He gave her a searching look. "You have still got the necklace, right?"

Orla nodded. "It's safe."

She was so tired. And her head hurt so much. "Let's go home," she said.

As they trudged in silence through Poldevel, it was Tom who noticed first.

"There are no street lights," he said.

"They switch them off at midnight," said Richard. "To save energy and reduce light pollution."

"You don't get it," said Tom. "There are no lamp posts."

"He's right," breathed Raven. She spun a circle in the lane, then turned to face the others. "You still don't get it, do you?" She laughed. "No parked cars. No tarmac on the road. And where's the moon gone? You did it, Orla. Your magic spell worked. We've gone back in time."

"Oh my God," said Richard, his hands outstretched as though he expected to fall over. "This. Is. Freaky."

Orla went icy cold. "I think that crow is waiting for us," she whispered.

The bird was perched exactly opposite the old vicarage. Except the building wasn't quite as old as Orla remembered – the walls that only this afternoon had been covered in purple wisteria were bare, grey stone and the

201

gravel she'd crunched across was now pure mud. She heard a clink of metal, the creak of leather and the clop of a hoof. Turning, she pushed the others into the darkest shadows, hushing them with a touch of the lip. Two horses emerged from the vicarage, one black and one white. On their backs, two men in tricorn hats and long coats.

Suddenly, the white horse stopped.

"Get on," growled the rider, but to no avail. Something had spooked it and, eyes rolling, it went into reverse. As his companion laughed, the rider wheeled his mount and tried to go forward again.

"You should get a proper 'oss, Vicar," laughed the other. "One that's not afeared of foxes." He tapped his horse with his heel and headed down the lane.

"Run," hissed Orla.

The crow led the way.

The four fled back past the church and into the field beyond.

Richard bent over, placed his hands on his knees and shook his head. "This is insane."

"No – it's amazing," said Tom. "We've actually gone back in time."

Orla shook her head. "You can't travel back in time. I think we're kind of sharing a dream."

"That's called atavistic magic," said Raven.

Tom held his hands up in front of his face. "So are we here, or are we asleep by the church?"

Orla looked at him for a long time. "I don't know," she admitted.

"What about those men?" asked Raven. "Are they part of the dream or real?"

Orla took a deep breath. "Dunno." She shrugged. "This isn't how I thought the memory stone would work."

"If we are in the past…"

"We're not back in the past."

"Yeah," persisted Tom, "but if we are, can we get back to the future?"

"I'm not sure."

"Christ," said Richard. "When I agreed to this I thought we were going to, like, go into a trance or something."

"Maybe that's what we've done," said Orla. "Like Tom said, we're probably asleep by the grave."

"Can we go and look?" said Tom.

"No way," said Raven. "How can seeing ourselves sleeping by a grave ever be a good thing?"

"Look, it doesn't matter where we are," snapped Orla. "We have no choice but to go where he says."

"Where who says?" asked Richard.

Orla pointed at the crow. "Him," she said. "The Man in Black."

* * *

Bucca Dhu led them across the field, west along a muddy track through a deep, wooded valley, then south, up a steep hill towards the sea. The great arc of the Milky Way flew overhead, its silver light reflected on every leaf and blade of grass.

Tom reached the top first.

"Oh my God," he yelped. He turned back to the others. "You won't believe this. There's a pirate ship in the bay, like the one in my dream."

A three-masted sloop lay at anchor in the lee of the cliffs, not a light burning aboard. A woman was standing on the clifftop: a silhouette against the sea with a basket in one hand, a staff in the other and a bundle at her feet.

"Is that Pedervander Mazey?" whispered Raven.

"Nope," said Orla. "Too short."

"Do you think we're actually invisible?" asked Tom.

"I think it's something we should probably try and find out before we approach the locals," said Richard.

"I was invisible last time," said Orla. "Only Pedervander could see me. Oh, and some maniac who tried to bash my head in outside the pub."

"Nice," said Raven.

Then, from the other side of the hedge, came a low voice.

"So you found the stone, girl?"

Orla pushed her way through the hedge. She saw the black dogs first, their eyes flickering like candles. Then Pedervander Mazey, tall, slim and somehow vulnerable, perhaps scared, even.

"Who accompanies you?"

"My brothers, Richard and Tom," said Orla. "And that's Raven. I needed them. Can they see you?"

Pedervander, her face hidden beneath a shawl, gave the slightest of shrugs. "Ask them."

She didn't have to. Richard and Tom were standing behind her, their mouths gaping. Raven was scowling.

"Is this her?" gasped Tom.

"What are those dogs?" asked Richard.

"The same ones that destroyed my camp," whispered Raven.

Pedervander pulled the shawl from her head and pushed her copper ringlets from her face. Her unscarred face. "My Wisht Hounds won't hurt you." She looked at Orla. "I'd say I was impressed that you had the power to bring company, but then you've got a lot of strength, haven't you, girl?"

She pointed her staff at the cliff, the old woman and the sea. "What you'll see this night has already passed. There's no action you can take to change it, but you need to see it. Out there is the *Phantom*. It's Cadan Leverick's ship. That woman there is my mother, Kathryn Mazey. Before the night is out, she'll lie dead on the sand."

"And you?" asked Orla.

"For my sins, I'll live. A menkolon and a knocker protect me. You'll see."

Suddenly, she was gone, striding through the wet grass to where the old woman stood looking out to sea.

"What is she talking about?" whispered Tom.

"No idea," said Orla.

CHAPTER 26

Pedervander stood beside Kathryn Mazey as the rest of them caught up.

"Who are these devils?" croaked the old woman, peering at the children.

"I thought we were invisible," whispered Richard.

Pedervander looked over her shoulder. "You are to them without the eye. But my mother's a peller too. Much diminished in her powers, but sometimes she can still see. She's sick and she won't be cured, not by me nor her own hand. She begged me to leave her but I knew what pain she faced if I left her. So I tried to take her with me."

"To where?" asked Orla.

"Brittany."

The cries of an infant pierced the night. Loud and sudden, like a car alarm going off.

"You have a baby?" gasped Raven.

The peller took the basket from her mother, bent and lifted out a shrieking bundle.

207

"I do, girl. Zephyr Leverick." She nodded towards the Atlantic. "Cadan's son." She turned to Orla. "And your blood."

Pedervander tried to comfort the child, but he just cried louder. "You need to hush, my sweet," she said, holding him tight against her chest. He ignored her. "Hush now," she urged. "Please."

In the darkness, the baby's screams seemed like the loudest noise on earth. Kathryn grabbed the child, held a claw-like hand over his face and whispered strange words. The baby fell silent.

"Come," said Pedervander. "We're late."

The dogs loped ahead, their hackles high and their noses low.

Orla jogged to catch up with the peller. "Why are you going to Brittany?"

"Because Cadan Leverick and I can't be together in this land. He's a pirate, an outlaw. I'm a peller and I bore this child out of wedlock, while Cadan was plundering the Carib. When he returned, I gave him his son. He gave me a fine necklace in return."

"The Nagasalohita," said Orla.

"We may talk of that later," said Pedervander.

Orla grabbed the witch's sleeve. "Oh no. We need to talk about it now, before you disappear again."

Pedervander shrugged her arm free, her face flashing with anger. "You don't know what you are talking about, girl. There's a way, and this is it. Tonight you'll see."

She turned to Kathryn. "Come, Mother."

Pedervander carried on down the cliff path. The track was getting steeper, and she was using her staff now to keep her balance on the path of mud and rock carved through the gorse.

"Cadan didn't have to wait. Everyone said he'd abandon me and the child – even Jack Kelynack told me that."

"Who's Jack Kelynack?"

"The man who spoke up for me in the inn. Cadan's trusted friend."

"Is he a pirate too?"

Pedervander smiled. "Jack Kelynack a pirate? Now there's a fine thought. He's not that kind of man. He farms pigs in Trewarthenick. He fooled himself that he was looking after me while Cadan was away."

She stopped on a rock, waiting for the others to catch up. "I do not recall it taking so long to descend the cliff. And you, sir" – she pointed her staff at Richard – "you do not need to help Kathryn Mazey down the path. She reaches the bottom quite safely alone."

"How long has Cadan been back from the Caribbean?" asked Orla.

"A couple of months. He came back, he saw his son, and fled before the constabulary caught up with him. I sent charms and blasts after him to protect him from them. He'll hang if he's caught. I heard he was hiding out in Bristol, drinking his plunder, but he couldn't escape his destiny. He knew I would always be the only woman in his life."

"Because he loved you?"

Pedervander laughed. Without humour. "Yes, girl, because he loved me. And because no other woman would go near a man belonging to a peller. Less trouble to jump off a cliff. I knew he'd return for me, and just four days back Jack Kelynack brought me a letter. We were to sail to Brittany. Pellers and pirates are welcomed in Finistère, and we would land there as man and wife, betrothed aboard the *Phantom*. So here we are. On the edge of land and life." She scowled at the black water. "The sea is no friend to a peller."

The dogs reached the beach first, darting across the sand like shadows.

"I hope he's worth it," muttered Kathryn Mazey as she stepped onto the wet sand, her long skirt dragging. Then she faltered.

"Pedervander!" she cried. "Pedervander, stop. There's somebody there."

Pedervander turned to Orla. "She heard them before

210

I did, and I told her not to worry. I told her it was Cadan and his boatmen. But—"

A sudden flash lit up the night. Orla heard the roar of the guns at the exact moment the musket balls tore into Kathryn Mazey, punching the life out of her as she fell. Orla saw Raven grab Richard and pull him down, as Tom dived behind a rock and Pedervander, lost and alone, turned her back to the guns to shield her baby. The Wisht Hounds sprinted, snarling, towards the riflemen as another volley flashed and cracked like summer lightning. She heard the bullets howling off the rocks and saw Tom run to Pedervander, seize her hand and pull her to her feet.

"Come with me," he urged. "I know a place you can hide." He took off across the beach, dragging Pedervander behind him.

Another volley ripped overhead, and then the riflemen started screaming as the Wisht Hounds tore into their ranks.

"Cover your eyes, for pity's sake," yelled one. "Don't look at them."

As Richard, Raven and Orla ran after Tom, two horses – one white, one black – galloped out of the darkness, their hooves kicking up spray.

"It's those men from Poldevel," cried Raven. "They're going to charge her down."

"Her Hounds will protect her," said Orla, but the peller's pursuers had planned for that.

Shaking her hand free from Tom's, Pedervander tried to run away from the sea but the horsemen cut her off, forcing her back to the water.

The Wisht Hounds darted past, froth dripping from their snarling muzzles. One hundred metres ahead of them, the black rider swung a cutlass at Pedervander. She screamed and ducked left, but the horsemen were faster, harrying her like sheepdogs towards the surf. At the water's edge, Orla saw her recoil, as if she'd stepped on broken glass. Blood was streaming from the slash on her face and as the first waves hit her legs, her Wisht Hounds vanished like breath on a cold night. She dropped to one knee and thrust her staff towards the horsemen, screaming words Orla knew to be blastings that would have been lethal had she not been in the sea.

Kicking his jangling mount to keep it steady, the white rider aimed his pistol at the peller's head. Orla saw the yellow flash a heartbeat before she heard the crack.

"She doesn't die here," said Richard. "Remember? For her sins, she lives the night."

As he spoke, the horsemen pushed forward, their mounts stepping high in the white water and forcing Pedervander deeper into the sea.

"Shoot her, Serjeant," called the white rider.

"Give it up, Mazey," growled the other. "Give it up and the child will live. I give you my word."

Pedervander's eyes flashed from one to the other, her hair plastered to her face, blood dripping from her chin.

"You have no power in the sea, peller," called the white rider. "Hand it over and I give you my word you'll not feel a thing."

"I know you," she cried. "I know you, Jasper Bates."

"Jasper Bates," gasped Orla. "He's the reverend from Poldevel. He was supposed to be nice."

Pedervander snatched a glance out to sea.

"Your pirate isn't coming, witch," taunted the reverend.

Pedervander was waist deep in the surf now, her right arm raised high to keep the baby dry. She must have seen the five riflemen jogging up in support of their master.

Reverend Bates turned to the serjeant. "I'm tiring of this," he said. "Shoot her in the heart."

The serjeant was struggling to keep his mare steady. "You shoot her," he retorted.

"I've taken my shot, sir. Better luck to you."

Spurring his mount deeper into the water, the serjeant pointed his pistol at Pedervander's chest. "Why don't you come out and put the child on the beach, woman? It's the best I can offer you."

"Do *not* let her set foot on dry land," barked the reverend. "She'll let all hell loose." He wheeled his horse, yelling at his terrified riflemen to hurry up. He didn't see Raven because Raven, like Orla, Richard and Tom, was what ordinary men call a spirit and what pellers call a tarosvan. A presence visible only to those with the eye, and to animals. Not all animals. Cows, for example, and sheep are oblivious to most ghosts, but pigs, dogs and especially horses are terrified by them. As Raven reached up to grab the white horse's bridle, all hell indeed broke loose. Its eyes rolling, the horse let out a terrible scream, reared up, and crashed backwards into the tide, hurling the reverend onto the wet sand.

"Wow," exclaimed Raven, as the white horse hauled itself upright and galloped away.

She turned. The black horse was spinning in circles, fighting against the bit and the serjeant's boots. Raven smiled.

The mare's eyed widened.

"Boo," said Raven.

The horse threw her head back, then groundward, jinking towards the sea. The serjeant nearly went over her front, but he was a better horseman than the reverend. He lost his hat but he clung on, just, as his terrified mount bolted, scattering the riflemen.

Tom saw his chance. "Come on, Peddy," he called. "Quick."

He waded into the sea, grabbed Pedervander's hand and dragged her past the rocks and out of sight.

Raven glanced at Orla and Richard. "That boy needs help," she said, then raced after Tom and the peller.

CHAPTER 27

A single set of bloody footprints led straight into the black mouth of a cave.

"It's that stinky cave Tom showed us earlier today," said Orla. "Raven and Tom are trapped in there with Pedervander."

Then the bad guys arrived.

"The she-devil's cornered," growled the serjeant, his pistol held at arm's length, a lantern at his side. He turned to the riflemen. "Shoot anything that moves, boys. We need that necklace."

The reverend appeared. Bedraggled, missing his hat and hugging his shoulder.

"Now listen, men," he began, wincing as he spoke. "Remember that tonight you are doing the Lord's work. You are not shooting a woman. You're killing a demon."

"Demons can't be killed, Reverend," said one of the riflemen, his eyes locked on the mouth of the cave.

"Yes, they can," said the reverend.

216

"Can't, Reverend," argued another. "Can't kill angels neither."

"Is that the truth?" asked the serjeant.

"For God's sake," hissed the reverend. "Are you a theologian, soldier?"

"No, sir, I'm not. But I know you can't kill a demon."

The reverend sighed. "Fine. Yes. You're right. We cannot kill the demon but we can destroy its human host."

"And that," said the other, "means we will be killing a woman."

"Now listen," barked the reverend. "If you leave this witch alive, then she'll take your wives, your children and put every last one of us in the ground. You have no choice. None of us do. Now get in there and do God's work."

Richard grabbed Orla's arm. "Do something," he urged.

"Like what?"

"A spell, for God's sake. You must have a spell for this, right?"

Orla gave him a look. "Course I don't have a spell. And Pedervander made it clear that she doesn't die tonight, didn't she? Saved by a knocker and a menkolon."

"What's a menkolon?"

"No idea."

Gunfire shattered the night. Moments later, the riflemen staggered from the cave, cursing and holding their heads.

The serjeant pushed past angrily, his eyes squeezed shut and one hand pressed hard against his left ear.

"She's vanished," he shouted at the reverend. "The cave's empty. Some idiot shot at his own shadow."

Then Orla and Richard heard another voice, from above. "Hey, losers, up here." It was Tom, standing at the top of the cliff. "The witch lady has run off. You'd better come quick."

It took Orla and Richard ten precious minutes to sprint back along the beach and up the path. Tom and Raven were sitting rather dejectedly on a rock.

"How the hell did you get up here?" panted Richard when he and Orla reached the clifftop.

"I tried to show you yesterday," said Tom. "You weren't interested. There's a secret passage from the back of the cave up to the cliff."

"Where's Pedervander?" asked Orla.

"She vanished," said Raven. "She's bleeding badly, too."

"We can't lose her now," said Orla, dropping to her knees and rummaging through her backpack. "I've got that oil of the moon. Miss Teague said it worked on bleeding cows, but maybe it works on humans too." She used her blade to lever out the tiny cork. The intense smell of frankincense and camphor briefly filled the night air as she poured the oil onto the base of her staff.

"Now what?" said Richard.

"Now I reckon we let the staff lead us to Pedervander. Let's go."

The effect was extraordinary – as though the staff were attached to an invisible bloodhound pulling her forward across the clifftop, down into a wooded valley and up the steep slope opposite. Suddenly Orla realized it was leading them to the top of the cliff where she'd first spoken to Pedervander. The fairy ring.

They saw the light first: the soft, yellow glow of a candle lantern. Then they saw the peller, standing in the circle of rocks, her staff pointing towards the sea and her dagger raised high above her head. Her baby lay in his basket outside the circle, while at her feet, coiled around her lantern and glinting with malevolence, lay the Nagasalohita.

In a low, strong voice, Pedervander Mazey began her incantation, and as she spoke, the wind rose. Slowly at first, but with rising fury, like a grizzly bear rudely roused from hibernation. It flew down from the cursed wood of St Ketherick like the blast wave from a nuclear explosion, screeching across the clifftop, flattening the grass, throwing gorse blooms like yellow confetti and whipping the flat sea into mountains of white water. It caught the *Phantom* by surprise. She'd already raised her rig to sail out of the bay, and the gale hit her like a runaway train, filling her sheets and throwing her forward with such force that the anchor cable snapped.

The whaler carrying the serjeant and his men back to the ship didn't stand a chance. Tipped stem over stern by the monstrous surf, it threw its screaming passengers into the sea, where wave after wave buried them, forcing them down and down again until all were drowned.

By now the *Phantom* was halfway across the bay, her bowsprit pointing first at heaven and then at hell as she rode the giant swell. Orla could see the crew frantically trying to drop the sails.

A spar snapped like a chopstick and plunged onto the deck, its canvas dragging in the waves. Now the rain came, thrown like slaps into the fizzing sea. Pedervander was directing the terror, standing in the storm pointing dagger and staff at the *Phantom* like a demonic conductor. The doomed ship was heading towards the sawtooth shore of Gull Rock, where the white foam looked as soft as clotted cream. Suddenly a figure – Cadan Leverick himself, maybe – leapt into the rigging, gripping on for dear life as the mainmast swung from side to side like a madman's metronome. As he cut loose first one sail, then another, they were ripped away by the wind. It was a crazy, desperate, heroic effort, but nothing could save the *Phantom* now.

The ship's back snapped like a matchstick as she struck

Gull Rock. She sagged, then, as startled gannets fled their roosts, the next swell lifted her high and slammed her back into the rocks. The hero in the rigging was thrown over the bow, his bones smashed on the black granite before he was sucked into the raging darkness. The hull crackled like a forest fire as it splintered, and on the third blow the mast toppled.

The screams of drowning men came through the gaps in the wind but Pedervander Mazey, her dress black with blood, never faltered. She was convinced that Cadan Leverick had betrayed her for those pretty stones, and she had turned their power back on him with lethal force.

When all that remained of the *Phantom* was broken oak, floating barrels and the drowned bodies of those who had set out that night to kill her, she lowered her dagger and staff. Her red hair hanging like snakes, her eyes black hollows in her face, Pedervander licked the blood from her teeth and turned to Orla.

"This is how it began," she snarled. "Do you know now what you need to do?"

"No," cried Orla. "I don't know what and I don't know how."

"But you do, damn you," hissed the peller.

Then she was gone.

CHAPTER 28

"Oh my God!" yelled Richard. Then, for want of an adequate alternative, he said it again. And again. They were back in the Old Ground, as though they'd never left. Thick cloud had obscured the moon and rain was falling.

Tom stood with his hands on his head like a man trying to keep a wig in place. "That. Was. A. Mazing," he marvelled. "I saved her – did you see that?"

"Oh. My. God," said Richard.

"I can't believe what I just saw," said Raven.

"I got her off the beach, up through my cave," gabbled Tom. "Basically, I saved her life."

"Oh. My. God," said Richard again.

"We've got to go back and see what happened next," said Tom. "Orla? Can we?"

Orla sat with her back against a gravestone holding her head in her hands, trying to remember every detail. Pedervander clearly thought Cadan had lured her into a trap and tried to kill her. He'd failed, and now he was dead. But it didn't add up.

"Why would Cadan have betrayed Pedervander?" she asked. "He loved her. He came back for her. He was the father of her baby."

"He also knew what would happen if he crossed her," said Richard. "Did you see what happened to those black dogs when she was forced into the sea?"

"The Wisht Hounds." Orla nodded. "They disappeared. The sea takes away a peller's power."

"So Cadan would have known that the beach was the safest place to corner her and get that damned necklace back," said Raven.

"Why wasn't he on the beach then?" asked Orla.

"Because he's a pirate," reasoned Richard. "No way he's going to risk his life when he can get someone else to do it for a couple of doubloons. He was probably watching through his telescope from the *Phantom*. It makes perfect sense."

Orla shook her head. "No, it doesn't."

"You want to know something that doesn't make sense?" asked Tom. "Look at the church clock. It's just gone 12.20 a.m. All that stuff happened in, like, five minutes. How can that even be possible?"

"It's magic," said Orla. "C'mon. We need to get back to Konnyck Vean."

"I'll stay here," said Raven. "I don't want to sleep in the Lightning Shelter tonight."

Richard put his arm round her. "You're staying with us," he said firmly.

As the kids crept into the house, none of them noticed that Dave wasn't there.

He'd broken out in order to do his job, but the operation had been seriously compromised.

He'd picked up their trail within seconds – the Surf Fudge Richard used on his hair smelled like bubblegum – and he could have caught them within minutes. But he was distracted by another smell.

Something floral.

Dense and sweet.

Perfume worn by someone deeply unsettling. A person of interest. But not a normal human person. A thing that made him want to tear flesh.

Sticking to the shadows, Dave advanced. The target was in the churchyard, moving left to right behind the wall. As Dave sneaked through the churchyard gate, he heard the click of a key in a lock. He heard the church door creak open and smelled a rush of damp, incense-infused air. The door closed with a soft thud and Dave trotted into the cover of the tower. All he had to do now was watch.

The church clock made a tiny squeak every time its hands advanced a minute. Dave counted eight squeaks.

He took a pee against the church porch, then pushed his nose low to sniff along the crack at the bottom. That perfume again, and something else. Something familiar and friendly. Not Orla, but part of her.

Malasana.

Dave's hackles rose. What the heck was she doing here? He sniffed again: it was definitely the doll, and that complicated things. Malasana was a member of the family, and there were two reasons for that. First, she belonged to the girl; and second, when Dave was a puppy he'd systematically destroyed every one of the kids' toys he could find. It was a necessary means of establishing his authority, but he had never chewed Malasana, because he, like the girl, could feel that she was more than a rag doll. He still felt that way, and that meant the operation had just gone kinetic – which was Dave's way of saying someone was going to get bitten.

As the door creaked open, Dave darted behind a gravestone. He watched as a dark, raincoat-clad figure locked the church, walked across the graveyard and concealed the key behind a tombstone. Then the figure turned towards the gate, and Dave could clearly see the carrier bag at the figure's side. Malasana was in that bag, and there was a drill for that: a swift and silent approach from the target's rear followed by a lightning-fast lunge at the carrying hand. The bag would be dropped, Dave would grab it and scarper. It was a tactic developed in the nineteenth century by a famous mixed-breed London mutt known as the Sausageer, and it was still devastatingly effective when properly executed.

His trot became a run and then, as he locked on for the attack, a dash. He hit the target's right wrist, snapping hard to trigger the tendons. There was a gasp, and as the wrist shot skywards, Dave released his teeth, landing on all four paws a millisecond before the plastic bag hit the ground. It was significantly heavier than he'd anticipated, but in this game you expected the unexpected.

Tail tucked between his legs, he shot through the church gate, swinging hard left and heading for the field. Unburdened, he'd have cleared the wall in a single bound, but the weight of the bag held him back. As he jogged back for a second try, he saw the figure approaching. His back to the wall, he dropped the bag and coiled for the pounce, wondering, as he did so, why he could smell burning.

The blast seemed to come from the bag. Dave had the vague sensation of hitting the wall and then the lights went out.

CHAPTER 29

Just ten minutes after falling into a coma-like sleep, Orla was shaken awake by a brainwave. She often dreamed brainwaves, which was why she kept a notebook. But this one didn't need writing down, because like all the best brainwaves, it was totally, blindingly obvious.

She jumped out of bed, dressed and crept downstairs to wake Dave. Except Raven was curled up where she'd expected to find a dog. That was when she realized he was gone.

She checked upstairs in the boys' room and then peeked inside Mum's room. She was still sound asleep, and Dave wasn't there. Then Orla spotted the mess on the bathroom floor, and the still-open window.

"What are you creeping around for?" It was Richard, his sleep mask pushed up on his head like a fighter pilot's goggles. "It's gone one in the morning."

"Dave's gone. I think he jumped out of this window."

Richard began to formulate a riposte along the lines

that dogs didn't jump out of first-floor windows, but, after what he'd seen tonight, anything was possible. He yawned.

"He'll come back. He always does. Get some sleep, for God's sake."

Orla shook her head. "No. Something's wrong here. How could we not have noticed he was gone when we came home? We've got to find him. Get Tom, and don't wake Mum. I'll grab Raven."

Ten minutes later, they were outside the cottage, equipped with raincoats, torches and the silent whistle that Dave pretended not to hear.

Orla swung her backpack onto her shoulders and pointed at Richard. "You take the beach. Tom, head up the hill towards the Lightning Shelter. Raven, head towards Boskerry. I'll check Poldevel."

"No way," said Tom, Raven and Richard at exactly the same time.

"We're not splitting up," said Richard. "It's such a basic horror movie fail."

"But we can cover more ground in a shorter time if we split up," argued Orla.

"That's what the girl who ends up dead always says," sighed Raven, wiping the rain from her face. "Don't you know anything?"

"Pairs then," said Orla.

"Nope," said Raven.

Orla sighed. "Fine. But we need to move fast."

They hit the beach first, turning left on the sands where they'd watched Kathryn Mazey be shot down just two hours and two centuries ago. They passed Tom's cave, then doubled back to scramble up the path to the Lightning Shelter.

Tom peeked inside. "Not here," he said.

"What if your dog came back in time with us but got stuck there?" asked Raven. "It's possible. He could have been in the wood and in range of your spell."

Orla stabbed her staff into the mud and strode onwards. "No," she said. "That couldn't possibly happen."

"Why not?" asked Richard.

"Because only people can go back." Please let that be true, she thought. Please don't let me have left Dave in the nineteenth century.

"Let's call him again," she said, so they faced north, west and east and hollered his name into the wind. In vain.

They crossed the field, climbing the hill and following the ridge to where it met the lane. Yelling Dave's name over and over, Orla clambered over the stile into the road.

Raven grabbed her arm. "You know we're wasting our

time, don't you? If he was out here, he'd have found us by now."

Orla shook her arm free. "If you don't want to help, fine. Go back to bed. But I'm going to find him if it takes all night. I'm heading back to the church." She whirled on Richard and Tom. "You with me or what?"

"Whoa there, tiger," protested Richard. "Raven's right. We'll never find him out here in the dark if he doesn't want to be found."

"What if he has no choice?" replied Orla.

"What do you mean?"

"What if something has happened to him?"

"Like what?" cried Tom.

Orla shook her head. "I don't know. Something horrible." She looked at Tom, then Richard and then Raven. She was tired and achy and felt close to losing control. And she knew they were right. Running around on a dark and rainy night in search of a small dog was a fool's errand.

Then she remembered the brainwave that had woken her up.

"I have to go to Menefrida Gloyne's house," she announced.

"You mean the psycho witch who's been trying to kill you?" said Richard.

"I remembered when I fell asleep. Mrs Spark said there

wasn't a parish record or ancient tome the professor hadn't read. She was the one who made the connection between me and Pedervander Mazey."

"And you want to go calling on her at two in the morning?" asked Raven. "You're crazy."

"If she really wanted to kill me, then I'd already be dead," said Orla. "She needs me alive because she wants the necklace."

"Nope," said Richard. "No way."

"Gloyne is the only one who knows what happened to Pedervander," said Orla. "She's the missing part of the puzzle. We need to make her talk."

"We're not the Mafia, Orla," argued Richard, wiping the rain from his face. "We're four kids. And she's an actual witch. Did I mention that already?" He looked at Raven. "Right?"

Raven thought about it for a moment. "I'm with Orla," she decided. "Sometimes you have to take a risk. Be a bit crazy."

"How does this help us find Dave?" asked Tom.

"Forget Dave," said Orla, immediately feeling terrible for saying it. "It's a waste of time looking for him in the dark. He'll come back when he's ready. Like he always does." She had an awful, inexplicable fear that he might not, but she'd used up the only potion that might have helped when she tracked down Pedervander Mazey.

"Where does the psycho witch live?" asked Raven.

"Polmassick," said Orla. "Behind a tall hedge."

"OK. OK," sighed Richard. "We'll go first thing in the morning. I promise."

"No," said Orla. "We'll go now."

"Polmassick is miles away," said Raven. "It's way out past St Erin."

"So we'd better walk fast," said Orla.

Raven shook her head. "Don't be an idiot. We'll take your mum's car." She looked at Richard. "You can drive, right?"

"Course he can't," said Tom. "He's from London. He's got an Oyster card."

"I could drive if I wanted to," said Richard loftily. "It's just that I choose not to for the sake of the environment."

"Jesus," muttered Raven. "I'll drive."

There was no road to Menefrida Gloyne's house, so they parked the car beside the yew hedge and walked down a brambly, nettle-choked footpath to a low, whitewashed cottage in a roughly mown clearing. Orla spotted the rock wall, overgrown with moss and stacked with charms. She heard the rushing of water and the rattling of wind-blown bones. She saw the dim light in a downstairs window.

"How do we play this?" whispered Raven. "Do we just knock on the door?"

"You stay here and cover my back," said Orla. "I'll go and talk to her."

She winced as her feet crunched on the gravel that surrounded the cottage, feeling like a burglar. Or a murderer. Glancing back at the others lurking in the shadows, she rapped on the door. There was no response so she knocked again, louder, harder and longer. Then, feeling like Goldilocks, she pushed the door, and it swung open.

"Hello?" she called. "Professor Gloyne? It's Orla Perry from the local history society."

There was no response. She had to go in. Digging her torch out from her backpack, she flicked the beam around the entranceway.

Three mice, encased in wax, hung before her, their tails entwined and the whole horrific charm topped with a pair of blackbird skulls.

Sparkle jars were lined along the floor, their snippets of coloured wool and ribbon radiating protection against evil. Candles studded with thorns from wild roses burned in brass candlesticks, and the air smelled of poison.

"Professor Gloyne?" called Orla.

A sudden rustle and the creak of a stealthy foot on a floorboard made her spin, her torch raised like a club.

"Easy," whispered Raven. "It's just me."

"I told you to wait outside," hissed Orla.

Raven shrugged. "And I chose not to obey." She glanced up the stairs. "I'll check she's not in bed."

Richard and Tom tiptoed into the cottage, glancing wide-eyed at Menefrida Gloyne's horrific charms.

"Oh my God," breathed Tom. "We're in a witch's house."

"Technically we're trespassing in a witch's house," said Richard, his hand over his mouth.

Raven reappeared. "Bed's empty. She's not at home, but who knows for how long? Let's find whatever we're looking for and get out of here without leaving too much DNA for her to curse. Tom, go outside and keep watch for her."

"And the cops," added Richard.

"This is rural England," said Raven. "There are no cops."

Orla flashed her torch around the room and let out a groan of dejection. The walls were lined with shelves rammed with leather-bound tomes, tattered hardbacks and box files with handwritten labels. Pamphlets, rolled maps and stacked newspapers were jammed into what little space remained, all guarded by a hypermarket of charms.

"How are we going to find anything in here?" she wailed.

"There's more in there," said Richard, pointing into the sitting room. "And upstairs, I'm betting."

Raven nodded. "Loads upstairs."

Orla looked at them in desperation. "How are we going to do it? All we've got are millions of books and the moon will be gone and this is our only chance to find out what happened to Pedervander Mazey and it's just ... it's just impossible."

"No, it's not," said Richard. "If she knows what happened to Pedervander Mazey, then the answer will be in there." He pointed at the laptop hidden in a canyon of books on the kitchen table.

"You're right," said Orla, making a lunge for the computer.

"What the hell are you doing?" hissed Richard.

"Taking the laptop."

"And turning trespass into burglary? No, you're not. We'll have to do it here."

"Wait," said Orla. She rummaged in her bag for the petrol station plastic gloves that she'd been absolutely certain would come in handy one day. "Here," she said, handing a pair each to Richard and Raven.

"I've got my own, thank you," sniffed Raven, pulling on a pair of black velvet opera gloves.

"Very elegant," commented Richard. "Now run along and let me do what I do best." He pulled up a chair, tapped the keyboard and groaned.

"Password protected."

"Is that a problem?" asked Raven.

"Shut up and let me work."

"Fine," she retorted. "I'll search her library." She dragged a finger across a bookshelf and glanced at Orla. "Make yourself useful, Sabrina the Teenage Witch."

Orla sighed and pulled out a book. *Paganism and Witchcraft in Cornwall* by the Reverend Thomas Whipple. She pulled out another. *Traditions and Hearthside Stories of West Cornwall* by William Bottrell. A third: *Speculae Britanniae Pars* by John Norden. This was useless.

Richard wasn't getting anywhere either. He'd been through the professor's cache. He'd searched her handbag. He'd scanned the room for reminders. He'd rummaged through the table's single drawer for an aide-memoire, and he still hadn't found a single clue to cracking the password. Then he'd rebooted the laptop in safe mode. Looked in Windows for the Credentials panel. Searched the hard drive for PWD files. And got nowhere.

Then Tom came in.

"You're supposed to be on watch," hissed Orla. "Get back out there."

"I got bored," he said, as though he'd been waiting for a bus rather than looking out for a psychopathic witch. "And there's no one about."

"Will you shut the hell up?" growled Richard. "I can't crack the password with you lot wittering on."

He stabbed the keyboard in frustration, his face shiny with sweat. "This is a nightmare."

"Have you tried *Trepolpen*?" asked Tom.

Richard glared at him. "What?"

"T-R-E-P-O-L-P-E-N. It's written on the lid."

Richard slapped down the lid, upon which a yellow Post-it displayed exactly those letters.

" 'By Tre, Pol and Pen shall ye know all Cornishmen'," recited Raven, opening a box file full of newspaper cuttings. "Old Cornish saying."

CHAPTER 30

It took Richard minutes to find the answer. Professor Gloyne's laptop had tens of thousands of references to Pedervander Mazey, thousands linking Cadan with Pedervander, hundreds tying the Mazeys to the Reverend Jasper Bates and just four containing the name Jack Kelynack.

"Why Jack Kelynack?" asked Orla. "He's just a pig farmer."

"You should pay more attention," said Richard. "Jack Kelynack kept an eye on Pedervander while Cadan was away. Soon as I heard that story I thought there must be more to it than a man looking out for his best friend's girl. It was Jack Kelynack who told Pedervander that Cadan was coming. He's the key." He tapped the keys and hit return.

"And there's the proof."

On the left-hand side of the screen a scanned document, handwritten in spidery ink. On the right was the professor's transcript. It said:

Herewith the last confession of I, Jacob John Kelynack
of Trewarthenick in the Parish of Tregony, Cornwall,
made this day Wednesday the twenty-eighth of
November in the year of our Lord eighteen hundred
and nineteen.

Cadan Leverick was my friend and I betrayed him
for the love of Pedervander Mazey of Konnyck Vean in
Poldevel Parish.

In June eighteen hundred and twelve Cadan
Leverick informed me of a plan to flee Cornwall
for Brittany aboard the *Phantom*, taking with him
Pedervander Mazey and their infant son. To my
shame I shared this information with the Reverend
Jasper Bates of Poldevel Parish, trusting in his
promise that Cadan Leverick would be transported
rather than hanged. I did so in the wicked hope that I
would then make Pedervander Mazey my wife.

On the tenth of August eighteen hundred and
twelve, the Reverend Bates and his accomplice,
Serjeant John Lamorran, sent a crew to storm the
Phantom off the Devonshire coast, taking Cadan
Leverick prisoner.

On the eleventh day of August I learned from the
serjeant that the plan was to lure Pedervander Mazey
to the sea, where her powers were weakest, and to

take from her a necklace of great worth. Thereafter, said the serjeant, she was to be killed. I set off immediately to warn her, but as I rode from Veryan I was taken into custody by the serjeant's men.

The Reverend Bates visited me in Tregony Gaol on the fourteenth day of August. He said Pedervander Mazey had conjured a deadly storm that had caused Cadan Leverick, John Lamorran and numerous other men to perish. He told me furthermore that Pedervander Mazey knew well of my part in the conspiracy, and that she would destroy all those who had wronged her. It was Jasper Bates's suggestion that Pedervander Mazey should be executed for her crimes.

In fear I agreed, but on my release I went to Konnyck Vean, where I found Pedervander Mazey mortally wounded. When she learned that Cadan had been innocent of betrayal she began to cry, saying that her broken heart had cursed the parish with the blackest of magic. This curse would be fed by the earth, growing stronger every hour and spreading across the land like the pox. Reversing it required the light of the full moon, but she knew she would not live that long, praying instead that one of her kin as yet unconceived – and thus innocent – would undo what she had done. Then she asked me when the men were coming. I told her they would be there soon.

"Then I must hurry," she said. "If the curse is to be reversed I cannot die by the hand of man. The magic will not work."

I urged her to take her revenge upon me, to which she replied: "My vengeance is to wish you a long life, Jack Kelynack. In return, make sure I live but one hour more."

I delayed the reverend and a drunken mob in the Poldevel churchyard. From there we processed to Konnyck Vean, with the intention of seizing the peller and throwing her from the cliff. The baby was in his cot, but Pedervander was gone. We spied her in the wood beyond, and chased her to the Lagasowmor well in Boskerry. At the lip of the pit, she turned and urged us all to go home. A blasting had been conjured, she said, and every man there present would perish before year's end.

All have. All but me, taken in drowning and disease and fire. Jasper Bates offered twenty guineas to the man who took her, but none came forward, so he alone advanced. He told her that if she gave him the necklace, he would spare her life. Pedervander told him the necklace was no longer hers to give.

Then, said the reverend, she would have to die.

Pedervander smiled. "I will," she said, "but, like you, sir, and all those here, it will not be by hand of man."

And as we watched, she threw herself into Lagasowmor.

Before sunrise this morrow I will join her.

"Lagasowmor?" asked Richard.

Orla Perry never cried, but she felt as close as ever to weeping now.

"The Eyes of the Sea," she sniffed. "That's where Pedervander went."

"She wasn't the only one," said Raven quietly.

The clippings from the *Western Morning News* were preserved in a clear plastic sheath. The first headline read "Navy hero took own life"; the next "Second diver found dead".

Raven dragged a chair across the floor. Slumped in it. "What was it that mad witch said yesterday? 'Suddenly it all makes sense.'" She looked at Orla. "She was right. Her brother went into that hole ten years and eight days ago. My dad's team were sent on a complicated search and retrieval operation on the twelfth of August. That's ten years and seven days ago. I always assumed it happened at sea. Not on land. But she recognized me. Lines of intention, she said. The coven knew I would come. They probably thought I was coming to kill her."

"These cuttings don't mention Boskerry," said Richard softly. "So you can't be absolutely certain that your dad was here."

Raven smiled, sniffing back the tears.

"Yes, I can," she said, shaking the document wallet. Two photographs fluttered out. Police cars. An ambulance, a fire engine and a white van with *Royal Navy Search and Rescue* on the side in blue letters. In the distance, the sea, grey like a tombstone, and in the middle ground, a yellow hoist astride Lagasowmor's mouth. Two serious-looking men in bulky dry suits stepping into climbing harnesses, one a tall man with a dark beard.

"That's my dad," Raven smiled sadly. "He went into that pit and it stole his sanity."

There was a long silence, then Orla picked up her backpack. "We end this," she said softly. "Right now."

On the clifftop, she hadn't known. But now she did. It was so glaringly obvious. Pedervander Mazey would never rest until she could undo the evil she had done. To accomplish that she needed the Nagasalohita and whatever was left of tonight's full moon.

"You mean we throw the necklace down that pit?" asked Richard, closing Professor Gloyne's front door.

Orla walked to the car and climbed in. She ached all over and she felt sick. "Yep," she nodded.

"I agree," said Raven, accelerating through Polmassick. Tourist cars lined the village road outside pretty cottages in which nice, normal families were sleeping in happy ignorance.

Orla looked at the dark houses in envy. She was so tired, but she knew there would be no sleep until this horror was over.

"Sun's coming up," observed Tom.

"Not in the west, it's not," said Raven.

"So what's that glow?"

A dangerous orange light lit the western sky, reflecting off the underbellies of the low clouds.

"It's a fire," said Raven. "Over where we walked yesterday. Must be a barn or something."

Orla caught Richard's gaze in the rear-view mirror. He looked as scared as she felt. Then Tom screamed.

"Stop! Stop the car! Dave. That's Dave!" He clasped his hands to his face.

It was Dave.

Or what was left of him.

CHAPTER 31

Dave's body lay on the edge of the road, his head hanging down into a culvert, the rain running off his coat in a steady stream. Tom threw himself down alongside the dog, staring into his lifeless face and gently touching his head, his ears and his neck.

"Oh God," said Richard. "He's been hit by a car."

Orla sank to her knees beside Tom. She felt as though someone had taken a blunt knife and cut a hole in her belly. Everything was running out. Softly, she took one of his rear paws in her hand. It was as cold as the rain.

Tom stood up, threw back his head and howled at the sky. "I hate this place," he wailed. "I hate it. I hate it. I hate it."

"Come here, Tom," said Richard quietly. He threw his arms around his little brother as Tom's sobs shook his body.

Orla ran her hands over Dave. He was already stiffening, but nothing felt broken. Carefully, she lifted his head from the ditch. His eyes were like scratched glass, his tongue swollen against his teeth. Exactly as she had foreseen in the horror of St Ketherick's Wood.

"He was a good dog," said Richard. The rain had stuck his hair flat to his head. "He was fierce and loyal and I think he always thought it was his job to look after us. And now this happens."

"Dave was too smart to get hit by a car," said Orla. "Think of how many times he did a runner in London and never got hit."

"This is the worst holiday ever," cried Tom, his eyes red with tears. He shrugged off his jacket and dropped down beside Dave. "We need to wrap him up carefully. Mustn't hurt him."

"Can't we take him to a peller?" asked Richard.

"Witches hate dogs," said Raven. "They'll save cats – 'a cat's never dead till it's buried', as the saying goes – but they won't help dogs."

Orla spun round. "What did you say?"

Raven took a step backwards, as though expecting a punch. "'Cat's never dead till it's buried'. It's what mad Miss Teague told us yesterday."

"Yes," said Orla, her heart racing. "She did." She grabbed Tom's arms. "I think I can fix this. I just need to summon the toad."

"But Dave's a dog," protested Richard.

"Just get him in the car," she ordered.

There was a circle down the road from here, next to a crossroads. She'd seen it while Raven was following her to Miss Teague's place – a neat ring of thirteen mossy stones beside the junction of two streams. A powerful source of sprowl.

Suddenly the night was lit up with blue lights.

"You said there were no cops," growled Richard.

"There aren't usually," said Raven.

"It's the fire brigade," sniffed Tom, looking out of the rear window. "Better let them through."

Two fire engines and an ambulance tore past, heading for the blaze on the hill.

"They must be going to Miss Teague's place," said Raven. "Bet she knocked a candle over."

Orla went cold. Miss Teague had known disaster was coming, but all those charms and protections hadn't saved Boskerry from the flames. She hoped the sad-eyed peller had escaped, but deep down, she suspected not. Just like old Mrs Perran, killed by a falling gargoyle while collecting grave dust. That meant Menefrida Gloyne had got to two out of the three pellers she'd met in the old vicarage. Just Mrs Spark remained.

And Orla Perry.

"Stop by the bridge," she snapped. She was angry now.

"You lot wait here. First, I'm going to save our dog, and then we're going witch-hunting."

Holding Dave under her left arm, she waded across the stream and gently laid Dave's body outside the circle.

Then she orientated herself within the stones. The west gate – Death's Gate – was seawards, so she was careful not to face it as she laid out staff, stone, flame and bone and the flat, black, desiccated toad.

With no broom to hand she cut a switch of hazel with her penknife and started sweeping, whispering *"Hekas, hekas, este bebeloi!"* to banish evil from the compass. Then she struggled to light the stub of wax remaining from the memory stone ritual, making a mental note to carry more candles in future.

If she had paused for thought, to consider for even a second what she was doing, all would have been lost, for in truth her conscious mind was ignorant of the ritual. But somewhere in her DNA, memories that had crossed generations were driving her actions, telling her to take the copal rather than the frankincense, the holly and the verbena rather than the myrrh and the rosemary. Then she intoned the same words of purification spoken by Miss Teague at St Ketherick's, the magic words coming unbidden.

She brought Dave into the circle and laid him as close

to the west gate as possible, where fat drops of rain fell like pebbles from the leaves above. She pulled the cork from the vial of aspercum powder with her teeth, remembering Miss Teague's instructions to mix it with a drop of blood.

Whose blood, though? Hers, or Dave's?

She looked at Dave, stiffening in the rain. What was the point of using a dead dog's blood? Had to be hers, right? Or maybe not. Maybe the aspercum needed to react with the victim's blood to work.

Drat. She was running out of time. She only had one shot at this. Dog's blood or girl's blood?

She could smell the smoke from Boskerry seeping down into the valley. A sudden gust thumped the trees, sending a cascade of water into the circle and all but drowning the candle. Sometimes, thought Orla, it didn't pay to think too much.

She took her knife and pricked her thumb, letting the bead of blood drip into the vial of powder.

The candle flickered once, twice, and then caught again. Dragging Dave to the centre of the circle, she held his mouth open with one hand and poured the potion with the other, careful to make sure it all went down his throat.

Kneeling by his side, she cradled his head, realizing

that if by some miracle this worked, Dave could never be allowed to know he'd been saved by cat medicine. It would destroy his self-confidence.

The brook burbled. Rain dripped, and from up the hill, at Boskerry, the whine of pumps and the faint crackle of radio chatter arrived on the wind.

Then the candle went out, the wick hissing in a pool of wax.

Orla shook Dave. "Dog," she hissed into his ear. "Wake up. It's time to kill bad people."

Nothing.

She shook him harder.

"Wake up, Dave. This is duty calling."

Then she flicked his nose. He'd always hated that.

It was probably the word "duty" that did it. Either way, first Dave's inner eyelids flickered. Then his tongue licked his lips. Then one eye opened, while down at the other end, his tail thumped three times against the ground.

Orla thought her heart would explode with happiness. Dave was back.

Then, rather tediously, Dave realized he was in the middle of a witch's compass, surrounded by magical tools and being attended to by a girl who had gone over to the dark side. Barking like a maniac, he leapt to his feet, jumped the stream and fled towards Boskerry.

Orla plunged across the brook, pulled open the car door and dragged Tom out. "It worked," she said, "but he doesn't trust me. He's done another runner. You have to get him back."

Tom nodded, wide-eyed, and took off at a sprint.

Richard gaped at Orla. "Really?"

She nodded. "I don't know how. Maybe he was just unconscious."

The ambulance turned out of Boskerry Lane, heading back to St Austell. Its blue lights weren't flashing and it wasn't in a hurry.

Richard shook his head. "He was stone cold dead, Orla. You know that." He shook his head again in disbelief. "My God," he muttered. "No one will ever believe this."

Orla gave him a stern look. "That's because no one will ever know."

Dave stopped running when he heard Tom's voice. His last but one recollection was launching a Sausageer special on a pungent old woman in a rain-lashed churchyard. Then he'd woken up in a screeching, hissing, roaring circle of darkness. And now Tom was calling him. He turned and trotted back – wary of seeming too eager to see the boy – but happy, as it happened, to be carried back to the car. Orla was there with her disturbing aura, and he had no desire to be next to her so he pushed across Tom to sit beside the window.

"Nice," said Orla.

Tom couldn't keep his hands off the dog. "I can't believe he's alive," he said, over and over.

Richard put his head in his hands. "Can we go home now?"

"You can," said Orla. She was shivering now, and aching all over. And her thumb was throbbing. "I've still got a job to do."

At that moment, the car conked out.

"Seriously?" said Raven. "Are we really out of petrol?"

"Looks like it," sighed Richard.

"But you've got a spare can in the boot, right?"

"Course not," said Tom. "We're from London, remember?"

"So we walk," decided Orla.

"Walk where?" asked Raven.

"First the church, and then Lagasowmor."

CHAPTER 32

It was a little over a mile from where they dumped the car to Poldevel Church, and they made it in twenty minutes, despite a south-westerly that punched like a bare-knuckle boxer. Dave stayed close, partly for tactical reasons and partly because he felt, well, not quite himself. It wasn't a bad feeling at all, but it was odd. He felt lighter on his paws, and more athletic, and the weirdness in the earth – the same fizzing vibrations that had fried his brains before – now seemed strangely comforting. He sniffed the air, smelling smoke and rain and evil. Maybe he was concussed.

The church clock was showing 3.25 a.m. as they huddled in the lee of a nearby hedge.

Plenty of time.

"Wait for me here," said Orla, "and keep watch. I'm going to get the necklace."

She climbed over the wall into the churchyard, and, keeping an eye open for spies, retrieved the key from Captain Hemming's grave.

As she let herself into the church, she noticed it no longer seethed with sprowl. And the font wasn't exactly where she'd left it. She glanced up at Malasana's lookout point.

Malasana wasn't there.

And then she knew: if Malasana was gone, so was the Nagasalohita. The game was over.

"It's gone," she said as she re-joined the others.

"Gone?" they echoed.

She nodded. "Gone."

"How?" asked Raven.

"How am I supposed to know that?" she snapped. "Someone must have seen me hide it. Someone else apart from you." She buried her head in her hands and let out a long, agonized moan. Apart from losing Mala it was the utter stupidity that hurt most. Or maybe it was the growing awareness that she had completely ruined everything. Pedervander had said herself that the curse would be fed by the earth, growing stronger every hour and spreading across the land like the pox. If that was true, then Cornwall, Devon and eventually the world would be turned into a toxic wasteland with no birds and no bees and no luck but bad luck.

"We were so close," she said. "*This* close, and now it's all over because I..." She shook her head. "And Mala's gone and..."

254

Raven put a hand on Orla's arm. "Moaning isn't going to help anyone," she said firmly. "You need to start thinking. How do we get the necklace back?"

Raven was right, Orla realized, and suddenly she knew exactly what to do. "I need to go and see Mrs Spark right now."

"Right now?" said Richard.

"I can't do this without her. I've seriously messed up and I need her help. You lot need to go home."

"No bloody way," protested Richard. And Raven. And Tom, all pretty much at the same time.

Orla took a deep breath. "Look," she said, "in the past twelve hours Menefrida Gloyne has killed Mrs Perran and Miss Teague. Now she'll be coming after Mrs Spark. And me, probably. You all saw the power we're up against. She could crush us like snails, so as much as I appreciate your concern and your willingness to help, can you please just sod off?"

"No," said Raven. "We're coming with you."

"Mrs Spark won't let you in. You're not part of the coven."

"I think we're a bit past checking membership cards."

Orla thought about it for a moment. "You're right," she said at last. She planted her staff in the earth, feeling the sprowl running through her fingers and up her arm, and stared deep into their eyes. "But you're tired, and you really, really need to sleep, don't you?"

Tom nodded. Richard yawned. Raven stared back.

"You all need rest," continued Orla in a low, slow voice. "Dave needs rest too, and someone needs to be in the cottage when Mum wakes up. If I'm not back, tell her I've gone to see the sunrise."

"Dave needs rest," agreed Tom.

Richard nodded. "You've gone to see the sunrise."

Raven shrugged. "Fair enough. See you in the morning, then."

Orla watched them until they were out of sight, then followed the lane to the old vicarage. The lights were out and Bessy still wasn't in her place on the gravel drive. That was a very bad sign.

Despite Bessy's absence, Orla banged on the door and rang the bell, over and over. The dogs in nearby houses had detected her and were waking up their tourist owners with their furious barking, but despite the cacophony, Mrs Spark did not come. Because, concluded Orla sadly, she was probably already dead.

Then she froze. Someone was coming up the lane. Orla ducked into the shadows, her staff poised.

"Relax," said Raven. "It's only me."

"Will you please stop following me to witches' houses?"

hissed Orla. "I sent you home with the others."

"You're just miffed that your spell didn't work."

"It wasn't a spell," said Orla. "It was just gentle persuasion."

"With a big dollop of witchcraft," said Raven. "But it won't work on me, Orla Perry." She performed a little curtsey. "I'm the menkolon everyone keeps going on about. It means 'stone heart' in Cornish. Magic doesn't work on us unless we let it into our cold, hard hearts. Thought you'd have known that."

"I'm quite new to this," said Orla.

"You're doing OK. What's the plan now?"

Orla was too tired to argue. She sat on the doorstep, wiping the rain from her face. "I guess we wait," she said.

CHAPTER 33

They didn't have to wait long. Bessy came down the lane a few minutes later.

"Orla?" cried Mrs Spark, a look of horror on her face. "What's going on?"

"I'm really sorry," began Orla. "But some terrible stuff has happened tonight—"

"Wait," said Mrs Spark, glancing around. "Not out here. Come inside where it's safe."

"Can I bring my friend?" That word felt odd. Until now, she'd not thought of Raven as a friend.

"Yes, of course," said Mrs Spark, fumbling with her keys.

She led the way into the kitchen, moving a stack of cardboard boxes and pulling out chairs so the girls could sit down.

"I've been at a meeting in Plymouth all day, then got dreadfully held up by a car crash at Liskeard. Is your mum coming to the car boot sale tomorrow? She seemed quite keen."

Orla noticed for the first time that the kitchen was nearly empty save for some paperwork, a few odd bottles, a kettle, a jar of hot chocolate, some old mugs and a carton of milk.

"I'm not here to talk about car boot sales," she said. "We have a more serious problem."

Mrs Spark looked worried. She sat down, pushing the pile of papers to one side. "What's happened?"

Orla took a deep breath. "Menefrida Gloyne has got the Nagasalohita. She stole it from the church."

Mrs Spark frowned. "The church?"

"Long story short," said Orla, "I found the Nagasalohita in a tree; I hid it in the church. Professor Gloyne must have seen me. The point is, she's got it, and we need to get it back."

She slumped into a chair, her wet hair heavy on her head.

"And Mrs Perran is dead."

Mrs Spark jolted as though electrocuted. "What?" she gasped.

"She's dead," confirmed Raven. "We saw it on the news."

Mrs Spark looked at Orla, then at Raven, then back at Orla. Her mouth opened, then closed.

"How?" she said finally.

"Hit by a falling gargoyle at St Michael Penkivel,"

said Orla. "And there's something else: Boskerry is on fire. I don't know if Miss Teague got out. We saw the fire brigade go up there."

"And we saw the ambulance come back," added Raven. "Slowly."

"I'm sorry, but I don't know your name," said Mrs Spark.

"Raven."

Mrs Spark raised an eyebrow at Orla. "Is Raven...?"

"No, she's not," said Orla. "She's a menkolon. But that's not important. The point is this: Mrs Perran is dead; Miss Teague is probably dead; and I think you're next." She sucked her throbbing thumb, looking for a moment like a tired four-year-old. "Or me."

"What happened to your thumb?" asked Mrs Spark.

"Cut myself."

Mrs Spark pulled back the sleeve of her cardigan to reveal a bandaged wrist. "Me too," she said with a wan smile.

"There must be a spell we can do," said Orla. "What about a blasting?"

Mrs Spark shook her head. "The moon is all wrong for blastings. And if Menefrida Gloyne has the necklace, there's nothing you, I or a hundred thousand pellers can do to hurt her." She pushed back her chair and rose to her feet, suddenly seeming smaller and older.

"But we must not give up," she announced, filling the kettle. "I know you're tired and despondent, but we need to formulate a plan; and yes, we need to act now before she packs up and leaves or, God forbid, turns her attention on us. The first task, though, is to get your blood sugar levels back up. You look absolutely shattered, the pair of you."

The distant clang of the church bell sounded 4 a.m. and a weary silence fell over the kitchen. By Orla's calculation she'd had less than eight hours' proper sleep in the past week, and her body felt like a wrung-out rag. She jumped as Mrs Spark placed two mugs on the table.

"What's this?"

"Well," sighed Mrs Spark, "I wish I could tell you it was a magic potion to give you strength and protection against evil intent, but I can't. And it would only help one of you anyway. It's hot chocolate."

Orla glanced at Raven. She was staring into a space somewhere between the table and the window, then met Orla's gaze with a frown.

"You OK?" Orla asked.

"No. I mean yes. Sort of."

"Drink your chocolate."

"Yeah." Raven nodded at Mrs Spark. "Thanks."

The wind rattled the windows as Orla sipped her drink, wondering if this was how soldiers felt before going over the top to face certain death. There was a stomach-shrinking fear, and an inability to focus, but the main emotion was just a stark, soul-wrenching sadness.

She saw Mrs Spark glance at her watch, but when their eyes met there was no smile. She simply stared back, as though examining a dead wasp.

Something was wrong.

"Take your time, my dear," said Mrs Spark. "We need to be sure."

"Sure of what?" slurred Orla, wondering why her tongue felt like a chunk of cold meat in her mouth.

"Sure that the hot chocolate is working. There's an added ingredient, you see." She pulled a small brown bottle from her cardigan pocket and placed it on the table. "Dried pollen from the *Brugmansia sanguinea*. The red angel's trumpet, from Colombia. Locals call it Devil's Breath." She picked up the bottle and studied the contents. "The active ingredient is burandanga: an alkaloid that, if you believe the hype, turns those who ingest it into zombies."

She looked at Raven. "It's not magic, dear. It's chemistry, and none of us are immune to that." She smiled. Then she frowned. "I'm sorry, Raven; did you want to say something?"

Orla tried to turn her head, but the nerves wouldn't tell the muscles what to do. Mrs Spark noticed. "Look at your friend," she said.

Raven was nodding at the table. Not at the table. At the papers on the table.

"Deeds," she mumbled, as though through a mouthful of frozen peas. "The deeds."

"Your friend's very bright, isn't she?" Mrs Spark smiled. "These are the deeds to this house. Here..." She spun the sheaf of papers round and pushed them across the table. "Have a look. This bit names the house: it's The Old Vicarage, Church Lane, Poldevel, et cetera, et cetera, and this bit says who owns it: Ms Patricia Bates – direct descendant of the Reverend Jasper Bates." She looked up. "That's me, of course. I've just sold the house to a smug little banker from London. We exchanged contracts in Plymouth today, but that's beside the point. The main thing is that my kin has been seeking the Nagasalohita since the sixteenth century, and then you come along for a week's self-catering and find it just like that." She shook her head. "That hurts a bit, to be honest. I'm presuming it was in that fallen oak tree. Pedervander Mazey would have chosen carefully. She'd have picked one that could bear the weight of the Nagasalohita. One that could both absorb sprowl and transport the negative energy back into the earth – and to think of the years we've all wasted digging holes and turning rocks." She let out a little sigh.

"Anyway, all's well that ends well. Which, I'm sorry to

say, it won't for you two. The Devil's Breath is blocking your neural pathways, in effect removing your free will. In higher doses it stops the brain telling the body to do the important things, like breathing, but I didn't give you that much because I need you to be able to walk with me."

She clapped her hands again. "Please concentrate, girls. You were never going to leave Poldevel, Orla, because you need to pay Pedervander Mazey's debts."

The lights flickered. For a brief moment it felt to Orla as if Pedervander Mazey was trying to intervene, but it was only the wind.

"It's not about revenge," said Patricia Bates. "Well, maybe just a little bit. Anyway, here's the plan. We're going to get into Bessy and go for a drive. Put your knapsack on, Orla, please."

She shoved the table hard, making the mugs jump.

"You're coming too, Raven. Don't think for one moment that I didn't know what you were up to. I gave you a chance. You should have packed up and gone home after my Wisht Hounds destroyed your little campsite, but you make your choices and you accept the consequences. Come on, dear, on your feet."

Orla's mouth felt like it was stretched into the widest, fakest smile imaginable and her ears were filled with a static hiss. She couldn't feel her fingers or her toes or even the ground under her feet. She followed Patricia Bates out of the kitchen, and watched as she opened a cupboard and dragged out a black steel toolbox.

She rummaged in the cupboard some more, then turned to Orla. "I think this is yours, dear."

It was a carrier bag.

Specifically, it was Malasana in a carrier bag.

"She's not a poppet but she has a certain charm," sniffed Patricia Bates, tying her headscarf and checking her lipstick in the mirror. "I detected the magic on her in the church so I took her. Didn't want her stealing my thunder. Why don't you bring her along and save me the trouble of disposing of the evidence?"

She turned to Orla. "By the way, hiding the necklace in the church was an astonishingly reckless thing to do. If I hadn't seen you do it with my own eyes I'd never have believed it. Like storing dynamite in an oven, you foolish girl."

Patricia Bates opened the front door, wincing as the gale threw a mixed salad of ripped leaves and salty rain into the hallway. She grabbed Raven by the arm, put a hand on her head and pushed her into Bessy like a bad cop mishandling a suspect.

"Get in the car, Orla," she called.

Orla didn't move.

265

"I'm getting wet," growled Patricia Bates. "Get in the car."

If Orla had been able to shake her head, she'd have done so, but she couldn't, so she simply stood frozen, clutching Malasana to her chest.

"Get in the car," yelled Patricia Bates, delivering a roundhouse slap that knocked Orla to her knees. "It's time I took you to the beach."

CHAPTER 34

Dave couldn't sleep. Something was wrong. He felt it as clearly as if Orla had bent down and whispered in his ear. She had got herself into trouble again.

He'd been pacing around the kitchen for ages, pausing only to sniff the draught blowing in under the door. Everything stank of trouble. Big trouble. It was time to make an executive decision.

He darted upstairs and jumped onto Tom's bed, poking him with his nose. Tom woke slowly, then raised himself onto his elbows.

"What?" he groaned.

Dave jumped off the bed, then back onto it, growling as he did so.

"What is it, boy?" yawned Tom.

Dave hated being called "boy", and he despaired of his inability to point out the bleeding obvious to humans.

"Do you need a wee?" asked Tom.

Dave hopped around a bit as though that was the right

answer, and led Tom downstairs to the back door.

Suddenly, Tom dropped to his knees and grabbed him in a bear hug. "I'm so, so glad you're back, boy," he said. "I'll never let you out of my sight again. You're the best dog ever."

Very touching, thought Dave, but this wasn't the time for cuddles. Just open the door, kid.

Tom fiddled with the handle. "Don't go far now," he said, but they were wasted words. Dave had gone like a bullet in the night.

Orla's last known position was the north-west corner of the churchyard, so that's where Dave went, sprinting down the track, across the road, through the hedge and along the field edge. Then he heard someone screeching Orla's name, and he ran even faster.

He arrived just in time to see the beige car accelerate out of the drive, and he fired a volley of barks in its wake, furious that they'd got away.

He looked at the house. It was dark, locked and empty. Something white lay on the gravel.

A plastic bag.

Dave pushed it open with his nose.

Malasana.

He grabbed the doll and took off in pursuit.

* * *

Patricia Bates, Orla Perry and Raven were half a mile ahead of the speeding Jack Russell.

"Can either of you row?" asked Patricia Bates, changing gear to tackle a sharp bend. "Come on: speak up."

"Scdts," mumbled Raven.

"What?"

"Sea Cadets."

"Orla?"

"No."

"Well, it's convenient that your friend is as sporty as she is nosy." She parked the car behind a thick screen of black-thorn, tightened her headscarf and emerged into the storm, throwing a sour look at the low sky. "Out you get, girls."

Orla knew where they were. The footpath ran past the back of Konnyck Vean, slowly descending until it joined the beach path just past the fallen oak. They would be passing close enough that Mum would hear if she shouted. If only she could shout. And if only Mum wasn't drugged.

Patricia Bates read her thoughts. Turning her back to the wind, she beckoned Orla. "Don't waste your breath, dear," she said. "See this?"

A poppet made of rough-stitched hessian lay in her hands. Brown hair tied with a lavender ribbon flowed from its head, and its mouth was a gash of red.

"Your mum was kind enough to donate a few locks of

her hair when I trimmed her fringe," she said. "The lipstick I found in the bathroom. It's all you need if you know what you're doing." She ran her fingers over the pins piercing the poppet's head. "See the red tops? They bring sickness. Black ones bring death. The lavender ensures deep sleep, so there was really no need for you to take my hops and valerian. Your dear mother will sleep until gone noon today, and when she finally wakes up and realizes what's happened she'll be wishing I'd used the black pins." She shook her head. "Oh, and this one's you."

The poppet was the same size as Mum's, decorated with red hair harvested from the hairbrush in Bessy's glovebox and fabric from the dress Orla had ruined at St Ketherick's.

"Won't need it much longer." Patricia Bates smiled. "Now come along before we all catch our deaths."

Half a mile down the lane, another rag doll was leading Dave to Orla. The magic radiating from Malasana was too subtle for normal human sensitivities, but as plain as a kick in the ribs for a dog. It took him precious minutes to reach the car, but now the targets were on foot he'd catch them fast. Then he smelled a human. Left flank. An old woman dressed in a long skirt, rubber boots and a plastic raincoat, a forked stick in one hand and a carrier bag in the other. Not the one he'd attacked in the churchyard, though. She smelled different and, oddly, Dave liked her on first sniff. He had no time for pleasantries, though. He turned to follow the kids' trail, but she stopped him.

"Dog," she called in a rasping voice. "Come here."

Heavy footsteps on the lane to his rear. It was Tom and Richard, gasping for breath.

"Dave," panted Tom. "Here, boy."

"Stay back, madam," warned Richard, stepping forward.

The old woman threw him an exasperated look. "Do shut up, you ninny. That your dog?"

"Who the hell are you?"

The old woman tipped back her head. Dave knew that look. It was that of a fighter.

"My name is Menefrida Gloyne," she growled. "You can call me Professor."

"Oh, Jesus," muttered Tom.

"He won't help you, lad. Only I can do that."

"It's the evil psycho witch who tried to kill Orla in the woods," whispered Tom.

"I can bloody see that," said Richard. He took a step towards her. "You stay away from us. I'm warning you."

Menefrida Gloyne looked at the ground, tapping her foot as though trying not to lose her temper. "For the record, I did not try to kill your sister in the woods," she said slowly. "Quite the opposite, as it happens. The lovely

271

ladies of Poldevel conjured something to scare her that would have killed her had I not been in the neighbourhood. And here I am again, still saving lives and getting no thanks for it. Now give me that dog. Don't make me come and get him."

Tom bent down, grabbing Dave's collar.

"Try it," snarled Richard. "Go on, try."

Menefrida Gloyne put a hand on her hip and gave Richard a pitying look.

"See this stick?" she said. "It's full to splitting with the darkest energy this earth can offer. I collected it under the waxing moon, see, and that makes it even worse. Now, with this staff and the right words I could turn the trees to splinters. That wall to powder. Your bodies to splatters of bone-flecked jelly. You get what I'm saying, boy?"

"Like I said, try it," said Richard bravely, taking another step forward.

"Attack, Dave," whispered Tom, but instead of going tactical, Dave trotted over to the old woman, wagging his tail.

"What the hell?" cried Richard.

Tom was aghast. "Dave's deserted," he cried. "We haven't got a chance now."

"Cut the drama, kid," said the professor. "Now, I know what you've heard about me. Wicked witch of the southwest. The incarnation of evil. Spoiler of milk. Terrible cook.

272

All lies. Well, mostly lies. Either way, you're going to have to trust me." She gave Richard a dangerous look. "OK?"

Richard looked at Tom, then at Menefrida Gloyne. "What choice do we have?"

"None at all," she said. "Now, I'm not good with mutts, being a peller and all. Is this one intelligent?"

"Not really," said Richard.

"Well, can he do simple stuff like fetching the post, or bringing a stick back?"

Tom shook his head. "He's not very bright."

The woman sighed. She held out her hand to Dave. "Give it here," she said.

Normally, Dave would have done nothing of the sort, but the woman was so persuasive that he dropped Malasana into her palm.

"What's this?"

"It's Malasana," said Richard. "My sister's doll."

"Is it charmed? Feels like it is."

"I have no idea what you're talking about," said Richard.

"Clever girl, your sister," said the professor. "Do you know where she is now?"

"Gone back to London," blurted out Richard.

"For a party," added Tom, unconvincingly.

The old woman sighed. "Family loyalty. How sweet. Well, I'll tell you where she really is. She's being walked down Tregastenack valley to her death. She's been drugged with Devil's Breath and the lass who was sleeping in the Lightning Shelter is going with her. If you want to save them you need to do exactly what I say. Got it?"

Dave approved. This woman was a professional.

She looked at Tom. "You: make a pentagram, and quick. There's hazel there."

"What's a pentagram?" asked Tom.

"Never mind. Just get me five twigs the same length." She thrust the doll at Richard. "Hold this."

"What's Devil's Breath?" asked Richard.

"Google it."

Dave watched, fascinated, as Menefrida Gloyne dipped into her shopping bag, rummaging through dried bones, parcels of felt, bunches of herbs, various stones and clinking bottles, finally pulling out a pack of tarot cards bound by a rubber band. She pulled a card from the centre of the deck, scribbled on it with a pen and thrust it at Richard.

Dipping into her bag again, she retrieved a bottle and held it out to Richard. "What does the label say? I haven't got my glasses."

Richard squinted. "Captain Morgan rum."

"Oh," said the witch. She pulled out another bottle. "This one?"

"*Physo* something," read Richard. "Your handwriting is really bad."

"That's the one," said Professor Gloyne. "Pure physo-stigmine, distilled from Calabar beans."

She opened a penknife. "Give me the doll."

Dave winced as she stabbed a hole in Malasana's chest, and pushed something he couldn't see into the cavity. Then she snatched the tarot card from Richard's grasp, rolled it up and pushed it into the wound. She snapped her fingers.

She really was very good, thought Dave.

"Sticks?"

Tom passed them over and watched as she wove them into a five-pointed star. She placed it on the verge, put Mala at the centre, pulled a third bottle from her bag and poured a drop of strong-smelling liquid into each of the five points. Then she stood over the pentagram, holding the knife above her head in a two-handed grip.

"I conjure thee, red spirits of the east road, keepers of the flame of enlightenment and the blade of cunning. Heed the call, hail to thee, awake, arise and be here."

The incantation went on for another minute – weird words in a strange language – before Professor Gloyne bent, picked up the doll and handed her to Dave.

"Go like the wind, dog," she ordered.

Dave knew exactly what to do.

* * *

The prisoners were almost at the beach by the time he caught up. By day it had been bleak, but in the dark hour before dawn it was terrifying. Huge waves glowed like ghosts before exploding on the rain-splattered shore, but the storm made it easier for Dave to move unseen. He darted ahead of the group, threading between the rocks, searching for a spot where for that one crucial second he would be out of sight of those in front and those behind.

At last he found it, and lay in wait. As the evil woman passed, the black metal box gripped in her hand, he darted out and dropped Mala. Orla walked straight past without noticing, so he snatched the doll up and ran ahead to try again.

Moments later, the woman passed him again, picking her way awkwardly through the boulders. Dave dropped the doll, and once again, Orla stepped over her.

This wasn't going terribly well, and Dave was running out of opportunities. Soon they'd be on the open sands. There was one more chance.

Leaping with catlike grace onto a boulder, he ran and jumped past the humans like a four-legged ninja. Crouching, he waited for the woman to pass for a third time, then pounced like a panther, knocking Orla to the ground. She fell on a bed of kelp, blinking in dumb shock.

Dave dropped Mala onto Orla's belly, licked her face, then disappeared. No one had seen a thing.

"Do watch where you're going," sighed Patricia Bates as Orla climbed slowly to her feet. "And pick up that stupid doll."

Orla did as she was told and Dave wagged his tail. Not bad for a dog who wasn't very bright.

CHAPTER 35

Sleepwalking, and with Mala held tight to her chest, Orla knew exactly where she was. This was the exact spot where Kathryn Mazey had been shot dead, and the route they were taking across the sands was exactly that taken by Tom and Pedervander. Out there, the *Phantom* had been at anchor. Here was the cave where Tom had spirited Pedervander away. And there was the boat that was hidden inside, already half afloat on the rising tide. Carefully placing the black box on a high rock, Patricia Bates pushed her prisoners into the cave.

"I know what you're thinking," she shouted, struggling to make herself heard above the storm. "You're thinking there's no way all three of us are going to be able to get this skiff through that swell. And you're quite right. Luckily, it's just you two who are going to sea, and the marvellous thing about this cave is that it faces directly onto one of the biggest rip currents on this coast. In the old days the smugglers would use it to get them past the surf to meet the ships bringing in the contraband."

She took Orla by the shoulder and pointed her towards the water. "You're probably feeling as queasy as I am being this close to the sea, little witch, but I need you to row this boat as fast as you can in that direction." She pointed towards Gull Rock.

"Now in you get, both of you."

Meekly, the two climbed aboard.

"Well done, girls," said Patricia Bates, "but it's only fair to tell you that you haven't got a chance of reaching Gull Rock. You're both strong-minded individuals, but the snag with Devil's Breath is that it stops you thinking for yourselves. So, what's going to happen..." She paused as an explosion of wind blew a wall of spray through the cave entrance. "What's going to happen is that I'll tell you to row, but after a few minutes you'll be out of earshot. You'll forget what you're supposed to be doing, and that's a twenty-foot swell out there. I honestly can't see anyone surviving that. It's almost as bad as the storm that killed those poor souls on the *Phantom*. It's going to be terribly sad for your mother, and while they do say time is a great healer, it really isn't. Only revenge will help."

Orla got it now. She and Raven were being put to death, just as Mrs Perran, Miss Teague and all those who had tried to lift the Mazey curse had been. She felt no fear –

just sadness. She looked at Raven's back and then down at Mala, feeling even sadder that she wasn't going alone. Then she noticed the wound in Mala's breast. The rolled card sticking out. As Patricia Bates pushed the boat from the cave, Orla unrolled the card.

The injured man of the nine of wands.

Scrawled across him: *EAT IT.*

Patricia Bates put her thin lips close to Orla's ear. "You're meeting your destiny, Mazey," she hissed. "Try to comfort yourself with that. Now off you go."

A wave lifted the boat and, caught in the rip, it raced through the shallows as Patricia Bates, standing on a rock, yelled, "Row, girls. Row for your lives!" Then she laughed, long and loud, as the skiff climbed a wall of white water and dropped into the trough behind.

Patricia Bates had told them to row, so they rowed, up and over the next green monster and down the other side.

Eat the card? Seriously?

Drenched with cold spray, Orla stuffed it into her mouth, then stuck Mala under her arm so she could grip the oar with both hands.

And then she felt it.

There was something else in Mala's chest, something hard.

"Row, my beauties, row," came the faint yet gleeful

call from the beach, the syllables half drowned by the thump of the surf. Orla reached in and pulled a tiny bottle from Mala's heart. Patricia Bates was telling her to row; Malasana was telling her to eat what was in the bottle. She couldn't do both, so she chose Mala, spitting the cork into the sea and tipping a bitter powder from the bottle onto her tongue.

As the skiff was sucked up the face of another wave, she grabbed Raven by her black hair, pulled her head back and emptied the rest of the bottle into her mouth.

Then she sat down and rowed, because she'd been told to do so.

Beyond Gull Rock, a set of waves born three days earlier in a dying hurricane in the western Atlantic had just arrived in Cornish waters. Over three thousand miles they had grown in height and breadth until they resembled a series of rolling black hills, two thousand metres wide and thirty feet high. As they funnelled into the bay, they grew taller still: a slum of cold-water terraces as high as three-storey houses – and Orla and Raven were rowing straight towards them.

Suddenly, Raven turned to face Orla, her face as white as marble. The physostigmine had worked and her senses had returned to reveal a situation that made no sense at all.

Then her eyes widened as though she'd just seen Death's

army arriving mounted on a million red-eyed horses. Orla glanced over her shoulder. The sky had disappeared.

"ROW!" screamed Raven.

On the shore, Dave watched as Patricia Bates waded around the rocks from the cave, careful not to let the rising tide flood her wellies.

Then she spotted him, stalking her like a jaguar.

"I thought I'd dumped you dead in the lane, you nasty little mongrel," she hissed. "This time I'll tear you into pieces."

She took her eyes off Dave for a moment to make sure the black box was safe. Bad move.

Dave charged, lips peeled back from his saw-like teeth, his eyes on Patricia Bates's throat. Still in the sea, a blasting wasn't an option, so she raised both hands to fend him off. Dave came through like an armour-piercing shell, locking his jaws on her throat. The witch didn't scream. Instead, she tugged at him with her flabby hands, spitting out strange curses. It didn't take long for Dave to get her to her knees, after which his plan was to turn her and deliver the death grip.

It didn't work that way. Instead of falling backwards, the old woman pitched forward into the surf, trapping Dave beneath her. He chewed for as long as he could, then emerged from the spume panting for air and paddling for the shore.

Patricia Bates staggered to her feet and stumbled ashore, blood dripping into the white water. The cur had hurt her, but she'd live.

Half a mile offshore, Orla was pretty certain that she wouldn't. They'd crested the first monster, the skiff going almost vertical as they rowed up its face, but as they slid into the trough Orla glanced over her shoulder. It was as though the Devil had put a mountain in a shopping trolley and kicked it across the floor of the world. Her shoulders burned from the effort of rowing, and as she felt the boat lifted by the second wave, she knew they wouldn't make it.

If she'd looked really hard, she might have seen Menefrida Gloyne watching from the clifftop as the skiff scaled a black wall, leaving a trail of white water in its wake. Close to the crest, it slipped backwards, like an unlucky burglar on a wet church roof. And if Orla had taken one last look at dry land, she might have seen Richard running down the cliff path and onto the beach. But she didn't. All she saw was Raven turning to face her, her hand outstretched and a sad smile on her face.

Then the wave buried them.

CHAPTER 36

"Lucinda Spark, is it? Or are you Patricia Bates now?"

The voice stopped her in her tracks. Panting, she stood in the shallows, one hand on her bleeding throat and another on her hip. Dave kept her at bay, barking himself hoarse.

"Professor Gloyne?" she called. "Thank God you're here. I think the Perry girl and her odd friend have taken the skiff. We need to fetch help, and fast."

She waded towards the shoreline, her eyes piercing the rain and searching the shadows for the voice. Dave saw her first: the oddly persuasive woman with the enticing smell emerging from the jumble of boulders at the foot of the cliff.

"You can stop walking out of that sea," called Menefrida Gloyne, "because what you're going to do is turn around and start swimming."

Patricia Bates smiled. "You look awful, Professor Gloyne," she said. "Have you been living rough again?"

"You should take a look at yourself," growled Menefrida Gloyne. "I'm giving you a choice. You can go out there and fetch those kids back, or you can die trying."

Patricia Bates took a few steps forward. "Or what? Will you blast me, Professor Gloyne?"

"You know I can't," said Menefrida Gloyne. "Not this close to the water. But come daybreak, when there are ambulances on this beach and a helicopter in the air and police crawling over Konnyck Vean, I'll swear I saw the whole thing. No magic in that." She nodded at the black box on the rock. "Is that the famous Nagasalohita? You happy now?"

"Over the moon," said Patricia Bates. She pulled a medallion from the neck of her dress. "This is the medallion that came with it. I thought it looked better as a separate piece."

"So you got everything you wanted," retorted Gloyne. "Why did you have to kill those poor girls?"

Patricia Bates waved a bloody hand. "The weird one was collateral damage. Wrong place, wrong time. But the little witch had to go. You know that, Professor. You may not have had the guts for it, but you knew as well as any of us that until the Mazey line was broken, we'd all be in danger whether we found the necklace or not. It was agreed long ago that we needed to bring the girl down here and drown her, and that's what we've done. It's a necessary human sacrifice and you know it."

"That was your plan, not mine," said Menefrida Gloyne. "I agreed to help. Not to kill her. Not to kill anybody."

"We made a devil's pact, Professor. We all knew that whoever found the necklace would have no choice but to destroy the others."

"No," said Menefrida Gloyne. "Only you thought that way. You could have just left us all in peace."

"Don't be ridiculous, woman," scoffed Patricia Bates. "Tying up loose ends is just good housekeeping. I've tidied up Mrs Perran and Miss Teague. You're pretty much the last of them."

She climbed awkwardly onto the rock where she'd left the black box. As she opened the lid her face was bathed in a hellish light, the red of arson, of splattered blood, of brake lights in a midnight crash. She raised the necklace, and it glowed like the lights in the Devil's own funeral parlour.

"Behold the Nagasalohita, Professor Gloyne." Patricia Bates grinned. "Is it all you hoped it would be?" She turned to Dave. "How about you, little mongrel? Can you feel your heart failing yet? Your lungs collapsing?"

Dave tried to advance, but it was like marching into a blast furnace. He started digging a foxhole in the sand, but Menefrida stopped him. "Dog, get here," she hissed, and Dave obeyed, staggering towards her hunched shadow. He felt as if he were wading through treacle while listening to white noise through headphones turned up to eleven and a half. As he got close, Menefrida Gloyne snatched him by the collar and dragged him to her side while furiously scratching a banishing pentagram in the wet sand.

"You're an idiot, Professor Gloyne," taunted Patricia Bates. "You and I dedicated our lives to the same end and yet when it came down to it, you really weren't up to the challenge, were you?"

Menefrida was on her knees, gripping Dave's collar so hard he'd thought he'd choke. The torment came in pummelling waves, each more vicious than the last, but through the red mist he thought he could see Tom clambering down the cliff. Barking to cover the boy's approach was the best he could do.

"Stop that noise," snapped Patricia Bates. "You're spoiling my show. Of course, I'm still very much a beginner, but it works exactly as the ancient texts described. You don't even need to hold the necklace. As long as you're touching the medallion and you can see the necklace, you can target anybody. Let me demonstrate on the dog." She placed the necklace on the rock and stepped away from it. "This will be the last thing you'll see on this earth, Menefrida, but I promise you'll be impressed. Are you ready? This is going to—"

She didn't finish the sentence because she was suddenly falling, hitting the sand with a heavy thud.

"See what you get for hurting my sister?" snarled Tom, glaring down from the rock where, seconds ago, Patricia Bates had been standing.

"I wondered when you would turn up," sighed the peller. She stretched for where the medallion lay in the sand, but before she could reach it Dave latched on to her wrist. The same wrist he'd torn into outside the church. It should have been a cinch to sever those tendons, but Dave hadn't reckoned on the effect of two centuries of sprowl on the old woman's body. She tossed him away like a tennis ball, then pulled herself to her feet, wiping the blood from her face and the hair from her eyes.

Dave hit the sea with a bone-cracking splash, but he ignored the pain and paddled back to the shore to launch a fourth attack on the old woman.

He heard Menefrida Gloyne scream, then saw Patricia Bates wiping her hands on her skirt as she watched Tom sprinting up the beach, the necklace still glowing in his grip.

"Silly boy," she called after him. Holding the medallion between a thumb and forefinger she counted down. "Three, two, one, *die*."

Tom fell as though hit by a truck.

"See?" yelled Patricia Bates. Dave hit the beach and

changed the mission priority: he needed to get those stones from Tom. Then he could come back and kill the old woman.

Tom forced himself to his feet, took three steps and was punched flat again. He pushed himself onto his hands and knees, but his strength was sapped. As Dave reached him, he collapsed on the wet sand, the necklace that was killing him gripped tight in his hand. Thumping waves of energy pulsed from the stones, blinding Dave and short-circuiting the electricity in his brain. Orla and Raven were missing and Tom was down but, as far as Dave was concerned, no one was dead until he said so.

Eyes squeezed shut, ears pulled back and tail between his legs, he darted in, snatched the necklace, and pulled. It was like biting an electric fence, but Dave knew that if he let go, he wouldn't have the strength for a second try. So he tugged and tugged until Tom let go, then dragged it seawards and dropped it in the spume. The pain stopped instantly, and he felt his life force surging.

Job done.

But now Patricia Bates was approaching, walking too fast for a woman of her age. Dave bit Tom's ear. They needed to find cover right now.

Tom yelped. His hand flew to his ear and he spun to face Dave, confused, as though woken from a fever dream.

"Where's the necklace?" he gasped. "I need the necklace. Got to take it to Mum."

Dave turned to face the oncoming threat. She was fifty yards away and closing fast. He fired off a volley of barks, then grabbed Tom's sleeve. The stupid kid had to move. Didn't he get it?

Tom started crawling towards the sea. "Need the necklace," he mumbled. "Got to fetch the necklace."

Suddenly a dripping figure loomed above him.

"I'll deal with the necklace," said Orla Perry.

CHAPTER 37

Orla should have drowned – a victim of what surfers call the three-wave rule. The first one knocks you down, the second one holds you down and the third one takes you down. By then, your oxygen-starved brain has accepted the futility of resistance and told your body to enjoy the ride. It's why it's said that drowning is easy. But not this night.

Grabbed by her hair, Orla had been dragged from death by Raven, not once but three times, and then Richard had arrived. Between them, they'd fought the suck and the thump to haul her back to shore, the blood streaming from a gash on her forehead. Most people would have lain sobbing on the beach, but not Orla.

"Get out of here," she yelled at the others. "It's me she wants. Me and this." She picked up the necklace and started running.

Faster than the wind, along the beach, through the rocks, and into the wood. She jumped the stream, passed the fallen oak and pushed through the dripping blackthorn bushes to climb out of the valley. At the top of the slope, she leapt over a stone wall and sprinted across the muddy pasture with its sterile grass. The western horizon still glowed red from the blaze at Boskerry and blue from the fire engines' flashing lights. Lightning lit up clouds like bruises, and the thunder exploded like an artillery barrage, the claps so close together that they sounded like one long undulating roar.

Orla was still running, downhill now, towards the steel enclosure around Lagasowmor and the tomb of Peder-vander Mazey. With a searing blue flash, a bolt of lightning hit the steel. An ear-splitting crack followed a millisecond later, and then another bolt struck with such force that Orla was blown off her feet. She landed hard, rolled to her knees and stood up. Another blow knocked her flat. Being struck once by lightning was unlucky. Twice was suspicious.

"How can you still be alive, little witch?" cried Patricia Bates.

Orla turned to face her. The blood from her head wound was stinging her eyes.

"I'm almost impressed," sneered the old woman. "You are one hard child to kill."

"And you're a liar," growled Orla. "You made out Professor Gloyne was the evil one when it was you all along."

Patricia Bates grinned. "Gloyne played her part like all the others."

"So you just used them," gasped Orla. "And when they stopped being useful..."

"I killed them," nodded the peller. "And now it's your turn."

"What about the curse?" cried Orla. "We could have stopped it poisoning the planet. What good will the necklace be when the world is dead?"

"Frankly, my dear, I don't give a damn," shrugged Patricia Bates. "I'll take the power and the wealth of the necklace and enjoy it while I can. The world can go to hell."

"You don't mean that," said Orla. "No one can be that wicked."

"Oh yes they can," countered Patricia Bates. "And if you don't have a baddy, Orla, no one believes in the goody."

She took a step forward. "Now come to me, little witch."

Orla gripped the Nagasalohita. "Stay back," she hissed. "I've got the necklace."

Patricia Bates wiped her hair from her face and sighed. "So you have. Well done. But if you'd paid attention you'd recall that the Nagasalohita cannot be used against its host." She smiled again, like she'd smiled that day she'd brought the saffron cake to Konnyck Vean. "The host is whoever is holding this..." She held up the golden medallion. "And that appears to be me."

Orla sneaked a glance over her shoulder. The steel fence

around Lagasowmor was three metres away.

"This medallion was attached to the necklace, oh, back in the time of Zenobia," said Patricia Bates. "Think of it as the remote control for the Nagasalohita."

Lightning struck the fence again, illuminating Patricia Bates like a strobe. And, briefly, the Jack Russell approaching like a guided missile.

"Without the medallion, the Nagasalohita is just a necklace. Pretty, but useless. I explained that once but you clearly weren't listening." She took a step forward. "Now hand it over."

And then Dave hit her, going for the ankle. Patricia Bates cursed, then spun round to blast the dog, giving Orla the time she needed. She climbed to her feet, lurching towards the Eyes of the Sea. She almost made it – after all, it was just three metres away – but a blow in the back smacked her into the splayed remains of the steel fence. No problem. She was close enough. But the necklace, snagged on the steel, wouldn't come. She heard Dave yelp in pain, then felt Patricia Bates's heavy foot come down on her wrist.

"I'll take that," she said.

Patricia Bates bent, unlooped the necklace from the twisted paling and placed it around her own neck.

"Now get to your feet, Mazey," she spat. "It's final decision time."

A shove pushed Orla to the very edge of the pit.

"The question they're all going to ask is did she jump, or was she pushed? What's the answer, little witch?"

Orla's heart was thumping hard enough to break her ribs. Her breath was coming in short, ineffective gasps, and she realized, with a terrible certainty, that she was out of tricks.

"Can I have a minute to think about it?" she asked.

"I tell you what, you irritating little brat," said Patricia Bates, leaning close to Orla's ear. "I'm going to count to three and if you're still standing there, I'll give you a little push. How's that?"

Orla looked around. A last vision of the world, with its thunder and lightning and flashing lights and hard rain and fire and smoke and crashing waves and...

"One."

...when she thought about it, there wasn't actually that much fear. Just that deep sadness, and the guilt, and...

"Two."

...then she heard Dave. It was a feeble bark, but at least he was alive. That made her smile.

"Three."

There was a thud, a gasp and the swish of wet fabric as Patricia Bates was pushed past Orla and into the hole. She made a lunge for the ruptured fence, grasping the steel with one hand.

"Will you people *please* stop sneaking up behind me?" she hissed, reaching with her free hand for the medallion. Before she could grab it, though, a green welly stamped down on her fingers, and with a terrified shriek Patricia Bates and the Nagasalohita dropped into the hellish depths of Lagasowmor.

A ragged figure with red eyes and a smoke-blackened face dragged Orla to the ground just as a searing blast of white heat burst from the mouth of the pit and rocketed skywards, leaving the sour odour of scorched air in its wake. It punched through the clouds, backlighting them like a death chapel window. Far to the north, high on the moor, St Ketherick's Wood exploded into flames, lighting the sky with a murky glow. The wind dropped, and silence descended like soft rain.

"Ding dong, the witch is dead," cackled crazy Miss Teague.

AFTERMATH

Orla Perry sat on the rocks, hugging her dog and watching the big red helicopter as it clattered overhead. She observed Tom, his hair flattened by the downdraught, waving as Menefrida Gloyne, strapped to a stretcher, was winched aboard.

As the crew of the inshore lifeboat turned back to sea, a young policeman approached.

"Morning, miss." He smiled. He was wearing yellow wellies, noticed Orla.

She smiled back. Dave growled. He was the authority around here.

"Was it you guys who called it in?"

Orla went for big-eyed innocence. "Called what in?"

"The accident. Lady fallen on the rocks."

Orla shook her head. "Not us," she said. "We just heard the helicopter and came down to have a look. Is she OK?"

"Hard to say," said the policeman. "She's in a bad way."

He gave Orla a quizzical look. "What happened to your head? That's a nasty cut."

Orla stared deep into his blue eyes. "It's a scratch," she murmured. "Just a scratch. I walked into a tree."

"And then fell into the sea? You're soaked through."

"Big wave," said Orla very calmly. "That's all."

"You should be a bit more careful," said the policeman. "It looks lovely but it can be pretty dangerous here." He glanced skywards. "Seems like we've finally got rid of that terrible weather we've been having, though." He looked at Orla. "Someone's worked some magic somewhere."

As he walked away, Richard and Raven strolled over and sat down beside Orla.

"What did he want?" asked Raven.

"Trying to find out who dialled nine-nine-nine," said Orla. Dave squirmed in her arms, so she lowered him gently to the sand.

"What did you tell him?" asked Richard.

"What do you think?"

Richard nodded. "Good. Look, we need to get out of these wet clothes before Mum wakes up."

"Yep," said Orla. Dave had limped down to the foreshore, scattering a huge flock of squawking kittiwakes.

"And we need to push your mum's car back to the cottage," added Raven.

"Then we need to get the hell out of here," said Richard.

"Amen to that," agreed Raven.

"We've got dead witches all over the place, a burned-down farm, a missing pillar of the community and a retired academic with serious head injuries. This place will be crawling with cops."

"Professor Gloyne won't say anything," said Orla.

"What about Miss Teague?" asked Raven.

"She's moving back to Slough," said Orla. She picked up the dog-eared red notebook lying beside her on the rock. "She left me her book of spells."

Tom jogged over to join them. "We need to get Dave to the vet's," he said. "He's whistling when he barks."

"Yep," said Orla.

As a fat August sun dragged itself clear of the sea, Dave waded around the rocks, breaking into a painful doggy-paddle when the water became too deep. He'd been sitting on the girl's lap for a while, watching the tiny bundle floating in the bay and waiting for the tide to bring it ashore. He'd picked his moment with military precision, and there it was, bobbing back and forth against the barnacles. Ever so gently, he took Malasana in his mouth and turned for shore. He'd brought five down to Cornwall and he was taking five home.

Mission accomplished.

The sea was like green glass, the sky was cloudless and there wasn't a breath of wind. Overhead, screeching swifts soared in pursuit of flies, and the kittiwakes had been joined by a flock of terns.

Life had returned.

It was going to be a beautiful day.

ACKNOWLEDGEMENTS

This book could not have been written without the guidance of my agent Kate Shaw of The Shaw Agency; the faith of Denise Johnstone-Burt at Walker Books; the patience of my editor Frances Taffinder; and the insight of my friend Jo Milton. And this story could not have been told without the wisdom of two Cornish wise women. Their names cannot be revealed and it would be inappropriate to call them witches.

They prefer the term "pellers".

C. J. (CHRIS) HASLAM is the award-winning Chief Travel Writer at *The Sunday Times*, specializing in extreme adventure. He appears regularly on the BBC and has written three black comedy thrillers for adults. One of them, *Twelve-Step Fandango*, was shortlisted for the Edgar Allan Poe award. *Orla and the Serpent's Curse* is Chris' first book for children. He lives in Cambridge.